THE DOMINO EFFECT

A NOVEL BY

ANDREW COTTO

Published by
BROWNSTONE EDITIONS, LLC
Brooklyn, NY

Cover art, design, and layout by John Passineau

ISBN-10: 0-61547-967-7
ISBN-13: 978-0-61547-967-5

10 9 8 7 6 5 4 3 2 1
First Edition

Acknowledgments

Thanks to all of the wonderful authors who have helped me over the years. Special thanks to my agent Jennifer Carlson for her belief in the story and assistance in shaping the narrative. My dear friend Kevin Mangini has tirelessly pushed me towards independence as an artist and spearheaded the book's promotional efforts with amazing ideas and energy. My father, beyond his paternal grace, brought the technical expertise and entrepreneurial vision to his son's reluctant DIY efforts. Finally, my beautiful wife Pam has been unwavering in her support of my dreams for over a decade. Every spouse should be so lucky.

To my Mother

Prologue

A famous writer once said that anybody who survives childhood has enough stories to tell for the rest of their lives. I survived, barely, and high school was the hardest part. Especially the last year. And to tell the story of my last year of high school, I have to start with the first year. Then the second. And the third. These first three parts will be quick and painful. I promise.

First Year

I had a lot of things going for me before high school started. I had friends, kids I'd grown up with, kids who met every morning on the sidewalk in front of my place. Every day, I'd take the lead by doing something nuts, like grabbing a watermelon from the fruit stand so the owner would chase me down the block. Or I'd have a seat at the sidewalk cafe and make like the big guys drinking little cups of coffee with their pinkies in the air. Once in awhile, out of nowhere, I'd drop a pack of firecrackers in the gutter and let the morning explode for a minute. Stuff like that. Harmless stuff. But good stuff, anyway, and the guys always laughed and followed me to the schoolyard, where they didn't mind when I picked the worst guy first.

We'd play all morning with just a ball and a bat and a strike zone spray painted against the wall. The same wall that held our names. Up top, higher than the rest, was my name: Domino. Everybody called me that even though my real name was Danny. Danny Rorro. I'd lived in that Queens neighborhood my whole life. My mother grew up there, too. She'd come from Sicily with her parents when she was 8 years old. Same house that we lived in. My father was from an Italian background, too, but from all over New York. His mother died when he was a kid, from tuberculosis or something, and he spent his childhood being shipped off to different relatives and foster homes. He was into music, mostly drums, and at 18 he joined the service and spent the next four years touring the world with the Air Force band. After he got out, he met my mother at the Roseland Ballroom in Manhattan, and she brought him home to Queens.

Everyone liked my father. He was funny and smart and what people around called a stand-up guy. He always talked to me about doing the right thing. About looking out for other people and helping them whenever I could. He talked a lot about his heroes, like Bobby Kennedy and Martin Luther King, Jr. I listened. I always listened because Pop was *my* hero. And I wanted to be like him, talk like him, act like him and everything. So that's why they called me Domino. Because my father's name was Dominick and, in Italian, 'ino' kind of means little, so "Little Dom" translated into Dom-ino. Everybody called me Domino, except my mother who called me Daniel, and my father who called me Pal.

And by the time Pop called me home for dinner, the summer before high school started, I'd been out on my own for most of the day with my friends. After playing ball all morning, we'd go to the pizza parlor and get slices with the money in our pockets, and afterward we'd go back to the school yard or maybe, if it was real hot, we'd go down to the shade of Spaghetti Park and watch the old-timers play bocce, or maybe we'd kick around the Italian Ice stand, under the awning, licking ices and talking a million ways around what was going on with our bodies, our muscles growing and our veins pumping with this crazy energy that led to the kind of things we knew next-to-nothing about but wanted more than anything in the whole world.

And even after my father called me home, and I had dinner with my parents, I kept thinking about those things me and my friends talked about under the awning of the Icey stand, and that taste of watermelon stayed with me through dinner. And the best part, the best part of the whole summer, was that after dinner I got to walk down to Genie Martini's house.

Genie Martini was the cutest girl in my grade. She was short and brown-eyed and had what people around called a great set of lungs. Her father was a plumber and into the races, so he'd be out most nights at the track. Her mother wasn't around at all, so Genie's grandmother came downstairs most nights, and Genie and I would share a love seat in the front parlor while Nona watched her programs in the next room. Under the blare of the television and the switching of the scenes, Genie and I would whisper in the fake light and touch each other best we could until her father came whistling up the stairs. I felt kind of invincible back then, untouchable, like the superheroes in the comic books I collected.

But all summer long there had been signs that something was coming. Darker kids with darker hair started to appear on their bikes, riding through the neighborhood in the middle of the day. And this was a problem because this was our neighborhood, and our neighborhood was supposed to be all Italian, so strangers weren't welcome. When they rode past the schoolyard, someone would yell "Spic!" and we'd drop our bat, let it clatter off the asphalt, as we chased those dark strangers back under the bridge.

The elevated trains ran through our part of Queens, and our neighborhood was separated from the next neighborhood by an overpass that, every couple of minutes, rattled over our heads. This was the border, and I, in all my life, had never set foot on the other side of that bridge. Stupid stuff, I knew even then, but the bridge was kind of sacred. So much so that all my guys supported this great idea I had to spray paint an Italian flag on the other face of the bridge, just so those from that side would know not to pass over into our side.

With a spray can in each back pocket, and one in my hand, I skipped Genie Martini's house one night and, before it got too dark, I climbed the stairs to the train station, slipped under the turnstile and sized up the practically empty platform. Down at the far end, with no trains in sight and no one looking, I jumped down to the track, high-stepped over the rails, and crossed to the other side. I ran down to the bridge, listening and looking for an oncoming train. I could see all the rooftops, and the clothes hanging between the buildings, and the skyline of Manhattan in the distance. My heart pounded and the sooty air stung my eyes and burned my lungs as I leaned over the railing and, as quickly as I could, sprayed, wide as I could, a red rectangle, a white rectangle, and a green one, too. I was so desperate to finish that I wasn't even sure if I got the order of the colors correct.

I dropped the cans and ran fast, fast as I could, down and across the tracks. It was hard to breathe after getting up onto the platform, but I kept running all the way home. Pop was waiting for me on the stoop. "Genie called, Pal," he said. "Wondering where you been." He looked at my hands and forearms dusted with fresh paint and my shirt lined with filth. Now he was wondering where I'd been, too. I told Pop everything back then, so I told him about the flag and the bridge and the kids we called "Spics." And he kept me in the house for the rest of the summer.

Pop taught music at a high school in Brooklyn, and he spent his vacations listening to the radio and reading books, tending to the fig tree that filled our patch of a backyard. Sometimes, one of his musician friends would come over and they'd play songs together. He cooked dinner most nights, too, because my mother had been going to college at night, summers, too, for the past couple of years. She liked it so much that when finished, she started up again, this time for a degree in law, which made sense because she could argue with the best of them.

Pop wasn't much for arguing. He stayed calm and listened when other people spoke, and he spoke nice and slow when he had something to say in return. He had plenty to say to me after that deal with the bridge. Not too nice and not too slow, either. I'd never seen him so mad. He spent the rest of the summer hammering me about the stupidity of my stunt and the stupidity of what he called "bigotry." He talked about history and the danger of us vs. them. He talked about Kennedy and King, those guys he liked so much. He said, over and over, people were people no matter what we looked like, and that he'd been all around the city and all around the world and knew this to be true, and that it was our responsibility to look out for each other no matter what we looked like and where we came from. No matter what. This went on for weeks, pretty much the same speech, over and over, so I was happy for school to finally start and to get out of the house.

Turns out the flag I painted was a tribute to some African country. And, in my absence, Genie Martini started going with some older kid named Tommy Destafano. Meanwhile, the big high school had big hallways and lots of strange faces. A couple of my friends went to a Catholic school and the others, still with me, seemed smaller and a little scared in the crowds between classes and in the noisy cafeteria that was about the size of a football field.

In the school yard, things were quieter. There was space and sky and games to play. But there was also something obvious, and that obvious thing was sides. There was an Italian side and a Spanish side. I guess there had been some Latin kids at the high school before, but this year, everyone said, those numbers had changed. A lot. And those kids riding their bikes in the summertime weren't cutting through; they were going home.

Immigration from Puerto Rico was on the rise, big time, and places I'd barely heard of, like the Dominican Republic and Colombia and Ecuador, were sending tons of people, too. And where they were sending them was Queens, and the neighborhood in Queens where most of the Latinos lived was right next to ours and running out of room because of all the new people. So they spilled. They spilled into our neighborhood and the different kids set up sides in the schoolyard.

Like I said, the school yard was quiet, but not a good quiet. Lots of stares and whispers, fingers pointed and posing. It seemed stupid to me, maybe because I'd made a fool of myself and then lost Genie Martini and my summer from that painted bridge move, and maybe, probably, because of what Pop had said, over and over, during those summer days I spent in the house. Either way, I wasn't having it, so I set out on my own to do my own thing. And that, I figured, was the right thing, too.

With a couple of our guys missing, we hardly had enough for a game, so I found the Latin kids who threw balls against the wall, too. Turns out those kids liked ball as much, if not more, than we did. They were some players, especially the Dominicans, and we had to divide the teams to keep things fair. Afterward, we all went our separate ways, but in the school yard we came together during recess and after school almost every day. No big deal. Just kids playing ball without sides.

The older kids, though, weren't into ball like we were. They stood their ground, on their sides, and kept inching towards each other. Things began in the hallways, where shoulders collided and pushes followed and, eventually, fights began to break out. Fights in the bathrooms, the hallways, and the cafeteria happened all the time. I stayed out of them and kept doing my thing.

Pop did his thing, too. He talked with the new neighbors

in Spanish, welcomed them with handshakes. People from around started to talk about Pop, and some stopped talking to him altogether. I guess they didn't consider him a stand-up guy anymore. Or maybe they didn't like the fact that he *was* a stand-up guy. Either way, Pop didn't care.

The school year went on and the holidays passed. Winter was long and cold and quiet. But things got noisy when spring showed up and the school yard suddenly had two sides again. The difference was that the Spanish side had grown over the winter. Real fights broke out. Fights with chains and pipes and sometimes knives. Kids were getting hurt, for real. Vincent Marino, from across the street, got his neck nearly busted and wound up in the hospital.

This was all older kid stuff, for the most part. Sometimes they'd throw our ball on the roof, and once in awhile they'd take our aluminum bat and keep it for a fight, but they left us younger guys out of it. But that was before Vinnie Marino got hurt. And before the day Pop had this little concert on our stoop.

I'd come home that day from the schoolyard and saw this crowd all around our stoop — little kids and their parents or grandparents spilling out onto the sidewalk. All Spanish. They were watching Pop, sitting on top of the stairs with some bongos, next to one of his musician friends with a guitar. They were doing that Simon and Garfunkel song about "Mama Pajama" and "Rosie the Queen of Corona" and everybody seemed so happy. I never liked that tune. I especially didn't go for it that day because while Pop and his buddy and everybody else were having a ball doing their thing, Vinnie Marino's friends were across the street, staring over at Pop with disgust.

Of course, they couldn't do or even say anything to Pop since he was an adult and we had rules for respect. But when they turned their eyes on me, standing on the corner, watching just like they were, I knew for sure that I was in for trouble.

Starting that very next day, trouble came. Every day, these older kids would spit on me in the halls and scratch clever things on my locker like "dead man" and "traitor" and "Spic lover." Real geniuses. And these bright guys waited for me after school, too. Most afternoons, around 3:00 in the school yard, I took a pretty good beating. The worst part wasn't the beatings, though. I got used to them. The worst part was knowing that the beatings were coming, and even worse than that was not knowing what kind of stuff would appear on my locker and who, exactly, was doing those things. It felt like *everyone* was against me. My friends disappeared, either moved away or afraid to be seen with me. My mother went crazy, talked to the people she knew, but no one put a stop to what they were doing to me. My father cleaned me up most afternoons and talked about sticking up for what I believed in. So I did.

I did my own thing, until I was walking home one day towards the end of the year and these kids come up from behind on bikes, but I didn't turn around. A few of them rolled past and I started to relax, thinking they were gone, when all a sudden, out of nowhere, something cracked off the back of my head. There were bright lights for a second and a clatter off the ground. The sound of an aluminum bat.

I remember lying on the filthy sidewalk, blood running across my face and into my mouth. It tasted like pennies. Dirty pennies. And that, for the most part, ended my first year of high school.

Second Year

The run-in with the baseball bat got me a week in the hospital and a shaved head. The wound was more like a gash than a cut, so they had to clear all my hair away to help keep things clean as it healed. Good look, especially for a kid, though I didn't feel all that young anymore. I felt numb, more than anything, and had this feeling that something important had been taken from me, but I didn't know what.

From home, I took all my tests and finished the school year. My mother finished law school around the same time, and Pop, the teacher, was done for the summer, too, so we got a bungalow at the end of Long Island in a village called Montauk, where the locals fished for sharks and rode the waves.

It was a long, hot summer of nothing. No fun with friends, no crazy excitement pumping through my veins. I felt the opposite of invincible (vincible?). My folks kept trying to get me to talk about what happened. And to understand that I hadn't done anything wrong. They wanted to know how I felt, but I couldn't really tell them that I didn't feel like a comic book hero anymore. Besides, I didn't really know. When I thought about it, no words came. So we spent our days at the beach where Pop floated past the surf and I sat on the sand, unable to swim and afraid of sharks I couldn't see. I felt afraid of other things, too, like the packs of kids kicking around town. They looked at me funny, in my sneakers and jeans and a hat I had to wear to cover my scar.

My mother took the train into the city most days to interview for law jobs. She came back soon enough with a position that started in the fall. But she kept taking that train out of Montauk, and she came back another day with news of a new house in Queens. She'd given up on the neighborhood where she'd lived since she was 8 years old. At first, she wanted to fight. I'd hear her argue with my father at night, dropping names of the guys from around that she knew – guys that she'd grown up with who were nice to us but maybe not so nice in general. She said they could find out, easily, who did this to me, and then they could make things right. But Pop wasn't having it. He was no pacifist, and he taught me, all my life, to defend myself. We had a heavy bag in the basement and he showed me how to punch and move, protect myself, which I did, best I could, for as long as I could. Pop just wasn't into the idea of payback, of sending another kid to the hospital. He wanted all this to end.

So when summer was over, we went back to Queens, but to a new neighborhood and a new house. It was a big place, too, looked like a castle, Tudor or something, three floors, stand-alone, with a driveway and a one-car garage and a shaded patio out back. We were separated from the neighbors by bushes instead of alleys. The neighborhood reminded me of towns I'd seen outside the city, with tall trees and green grass. People passed but didn't stop to talk.

I took a room on the very top floor, with slanted walls, a little stained-glass window and a spot to sit under the widow's peak. I'd be in the window most of the day, slouched with my feet on the opposite wall, playing Springsteen CDs and reading comic books in the colored light. My parents would come up once in awhile to check on me. Make sure I was OK. I wasn't. But they didn't know how bad it was. They kept saying things would be normal for me again once school started.

I went to a Catholic school, pretty close to home. I hated the place right away — way too strict and the only girls around were nuns — and those nuns could give those older kids from the neighborhood a pretty good fight. I kept to myself. At some point, in the middle of the first semester, I stopped speaking altogether, which drove the nuns crazy. They'd ask me questions in class and I'd just sit there, silent. So after school, they'd put me on the roof to clean out garbage cans as punishment for *not* saying anything. Nuns. One day, after throwing everything I could get my hands on from the roof into the teacher's parking lot, I ran home, straight to the garage. Pop had band practice that day, and Ma worked late every day. We'd moved the heavy bag there, to the one-car garage, and I punched it with my bare hands, moving the weight around pretty good. Through heavy breathing, I could hear the tear of my knuckles across the canvas. Pale spots began to show up on the bag, and I decided to cover the thing with my blood.

After the canvas bag was good and polka-dotted, I sat on a crate and ripped off the stupid sweater and shirt they made us wear at school. Sweat dripped off my chin. My knuckles throbbed and burned red like they'd been dragged over sandpaper. It felt kind of good, but not good enough. I walked up to the garage door and punched out a window pane. The sound of shattered glass, and the slashing of my hands, got me what I wanted. I punched out all the rest of them, too, sending glass everywhere. Afterward, it looked like my fist had been rammed in a blender.

My hand gushed and I watched it bleed, letting the blood drip to the floor. For some reason, I'd wanted to feel and see myself bleed again. I licked a wound and tasted the dirty pennies.

A puddle of blood formed on the floor between my feet. Then I wrapped my hand in the school sweater and went inside. With a pack of my mother's smokes, I went to the attic, sat in the colored window and sucked cigarette after cigarette until my tongue blistered.

Later, I heard the sound of someone coming upstairs. Pop showed up in the doorway and wiped away the air. "Have you been smoking in here, young man?" he asked in this hokey voice. Then he saw my hand.

He dragged me to the hospital. Afterward, I ended up at a different kind of doctor. But not at first. At first, I went ballistic at home. All that I'd been holding in came pouring out, and I was a long way from silent. Pop and I fought almost every night, nearly coming to blows on a couple of occasions. I'd cost him his cool, and there was something satisfying in that. Something small, though, I had to admit.

Eventually, I cooled down and cursed him quietly, letting him know through silence that I hated him. I blamed Pop for everything that happened. It had sort of come to me slowly over the summer and then through the school year and in the silence of my room; then in a rush as I sat there bleeding in the garage. The words I couldn't find came out in anger toward Pop. I figured if I hadn't gone along with his helping-people routine... if I hadn't listened to him and been his son... if I hadn't put so much faith in him and in doing the right thing, and hadn't told him the truth about the Spics and the bridge, I'd still be back in the old neighborhood, with my old friends, and Genie Martini with her great set of lungs, instead of being alone in the attic, attending some crappy Catholic school where there were no girls and not a friend in the world. I'd finally figured out what was bothering me, what had been taken away, and the fact of it was this: Pop had cost me my chance at being a kid.

Not a runny-nosed kid with untied shoes, but a real kid who did all the things I had been doing, with girls and friends and whatnot, until Pop and his philosophy of doing the right thing took it all away.

My mother was in the middle. Pop railed at her that I needed to get straightened out, but she worried about her son. Usually, growing up, she was the tough one, but with this noise between me and Pop, she tried to stay calm, begging me to behave before Pop did something crazy like toss me out of the house.

I think the counseling was her idea. I fought it, of course. Un-uh. No way. Un-uh. But they gave me two choices: the psychologist or military school. And while the idea of going away was tempting, it wasn't going to be some place with all guys, where you get your head shaved at night (my hair had just grown back) and your face chewed off all day. I'd rather stay at home with Pop and the nuns, so I passed on the drill sergeant and took the head doctor instead.

Not a bad guy, Dr. DeFuso. His house off Queens Boulevard had an office around the side. It was very brown in there, with slanted shades and a wooden desk and lots of books on shelves. We sat across from each other in cushioned chairs and he held a notepad and pen across his thighs. He asked me little questions that were supposed to have answers worth writing down. At first, I hardly said anything. But then I started giving him something to put on his pad, nothing monumental or nothing, but enough to keep me out of another crew cut.

This guy DeFuso was no miracle worker, but talking to him once a week for a few months made things easier at home. Pop and I still had our moments, but we had our peace for the most part. The best thing about going to the shrink was his suggestion that boarding school might be good for me. He talked to my parents, and one night they came up to my room with these brochures with pictures of nice looking kids studying and playing sports, posing with their arms around each other's shoulders. It seemed so safe. So easy. I remember holding the brochures and thinking, *yeah, yeah, I can do this.*

So we went out for a visit. Took the car straight across Jersey, past fields and rolling hills, past exit signs for places ending in "burg" or "ville." We glided down a winding road into a half-assed town called Hamdenville. Outside of town, we went through a high gate and up a higher hill onto the campus of Hamden Academy. Ivy covered the stone and brick buildings, and tall, tall trees threw shadows over the road. The air smelled new.

Some happy kid named Brian gave us a tour and, more than anything, I remember him saying "hi" or "hello" to a lot of the people we passed: Hi, Scott. Hi, Stephanie. Hi, Karen. Hello, Mr. Taylor. I wondered which ones would be my teachers, my friends. When we went into the underclass dorm, up to the floor for juniors, I picked out a room that I hoped would be mine.

There were some meetings with admissions people and a guidance guy. I met the baseball coach, too. But my mind was made up before any of them even opened their mouths. On the car ride home to Queens, I fell asleep and dreamed of myself somewhere else.

Third Year

That next year, on my first day of school at Hamden Academy, I walked around campus like I already belonged. I didn't really know where I was going or anything, but it felt like I did. It must have been all the time I spent that summer imagining myself there. And once there for real, I liked it right away. *These private school kids got it made,* I decided, walking under the high ceiling of the academic building, amongst all the fresh faces.

One face, in particular, stood out right away. I remember seeing her from across a classroom: deep auburn hair and a freckled nose, eyes that glowed green. Her eyebrows were the color of caramel. Her mouth was wide and, I could tell, easy to make smile. There wasn't this "Ah, Ah, Ah..." soundtrack playing or anything, and she didn't cruise up like a vision of the Venus on a clam shell painting they had at Catholic school, but the sight of this girl was like a miracle to me. I swear. I gave her a nickname on the spot: "Bella Faccia" for her beautiful face.

Each day, I moved closer and closer, row by row, desk by desk. I felt like a secret agent. After a week, I settled in right next to her. I sat up straight, caught my breath, and started to think of something clever to say. When I turned to deliver, she was waiting for me.

"So," she said. "You finally made it."

I almost fell over.

Through class, I tried and tried to keep my head straight ahead, but couldn't help but sneak a thousand peeks. Afterward, on the way to next period, I worked the little routine I had used for charming the girls back in Queens:

"So," I began, "tell me your name." (Brenda Divine)

"Where are you from, Brenda Divine?" (Connecticut)

"Do you like it there?" (Yes)

"Do you like it here?" (So far)

"Do you like me so far?" (*giggles*)

"Who's your favorite singer?" (Prince)

"What about Bruce Springsteen?" (Well, only "Thunder Road," but I've listened to it, like, a thousand times)

"What do you want to be when you grow up?" (A doctor or a teacher)

"Where do you want to go to school?" (NYU)

"Who's your favorite player on the Mets?" (Umm...pass)

"All right. One last question," I said, leaning into the door frame of her next class.

"OK," she giggled some more, hugging her books.

"What are we doing Saturday night?"

She smiled, but there was this sideways-thing with her mouth that cut that grin in half. "Well, actually," she said, "I'm taking the bus to meet my parents in the city, and my...my boyfriend's coming, too."

"Ohhh!" I cried from the boyfriend-bomb but still managed to keep my cool. "Can I come, too?" I asked. "I'm from the city. I could show you guys around."

"Maybe some other time," she laughed and walked into class.

She had a bouncy step and her right foot pigeon-toed a little, giving the impression she might be clumsy or something until you saw what a jackrabbit she was on the soccer field (I never missed a game that fall). I watched her skinny legs moving in fresh blue jeans. As she turned to slip into the seat, I envied the fuzzy sweater that hugged her slender upper body. Once seated, she tilted her head toward the doorway, blinked a few times, then smiled at me with surprise.

"How about next Saturday?" I asked. "You free then?"

There was something in her dimpled smile. Something I didn't know for sure, except that it was something I needed more than anything in the whole world. I swear.

Boyfriend or not, I sat next to her in class every day, taking the same walk down the same hallway afterward. We hung out after school and in the evenings, too.

I met other people. My roommate was a good guy named Sam Soifer, sort of a pale kid, always in need of a shave, with a body that drooped toward the floor like the *bazoombas* of a big old lady. Sammie had been at Hamden Academy for a year before me, and he took real pride in showing me around. He made it his job to point out everything and everyone he knew. It was kind of nice, at first, but it got old fast, especially after some kid asked him, as we walked through the common area of the dorm, "Hey, Soifer. When you crap, does he wipe?" *Good one*, I thought, but I also thought that I should find some other people to hang out with besides Sammie.

The guys next door seemed kind of cool. They played music and talked all the time about "*Bettys*" (which I figured out, soon enough, to mean "girls"). One was a loudmouthed kid, skinny with freckles, orange hair and a ton of confidence, like he didn't know he was a skinny, freckled kid with orange hair. His roommate played the guitar, playing the part of musician with a piled-up hairstyle, sandpaper stubble on his cheeks and chin, and the right clothes faded and unbuttoned in all the right places.

Those guys, Geoff Meeks and Johnny Grohl, started talking me up in the bathroom and in the halls. They would knock on our door, sometimes, and ask me to come over and "hang." They knew Sammie, like a lot of people, but, like a lot of people, they didn't seem all that crazy about him. And they never asked him to come over with me.

One day, on my way next door, Sammie whispered "Don't go." It nearly broke my heart, hearing him beg me like that, but I wasn't the same kid anymore who brought everyone along and picked the worst guy first. A lot of good that had done. It had cost me everything and got me nowhere. And I had some catching up do with a lot of things. So when Sammie begged me to stay, my heart might have stopped, but I kept walking.

Meeks and Grohl had another friend. A real cool guy named Todd Brooks. He was a prefect on the underclass floor of our dorm and always upstairs with Meeks and Grohl. Todd had some serious manners, wavy hair and broad shoulders, too. If we had a football team, he'd have been the quarterback; instead, he destroyed people in soccer and lacrosse. I learned, soon enough, that ours was a school of small circles, with no real center, but I was pretty happy to be in with those guys. They were about as cool as it got at Hamden Academy.

And Todd Brooks was the coolest of all. He wasn't just any old student. He'd been there since freshman year – which was something on its own, since kids came and went all the time. He also served as the big man around campus, at least of the non-wrestlers — our only major sport — which made this guy Todd even more important, because the wrestlers were about as charming as vomit. And with Todd Brooks in the lead, the four of us made our presence known around campus.

"Here comes your girlfriend," Meeks would crack whenever Brenda Divine approached my new group of friends. I loved the way she would slide into our booth in The Can (the makeshift soda shop on campus), help herself to a handful of French fries, and join the conversation. She was smarter than rest of us put together. Sometimes she'd challenge me to Foosball in the game area up the stairs. And we'd play for hours, spinning those little plastic men.

"You score there yet, *Paesano*?" Grohl would ask when I came down for more quarters.

"Get bent, all of ya'," I'd say every time, but I wasn't talking to Todd.

Todd knew my plans for Brenda. I was waiting for her and her boyfriend to break up. That's it. There were other girls around, but she was my Springsteen. I didn't like anybody else. We talked about it all the time, Todd and I. We talked about everything. I even told him about what happened to me back home. He was my guy, my buddy, my friend. My pal. We hung with Meeks and Grohl, but when it was time to divide, they went their way and we went ours. Until Todd went away with Brenda. And that hurt a hell of a lot more than getting hit in the head with a baseball bat.

It had to have been lacrosse in the springtime. They both played, and the teams traveled together. So somewhere, I figured, on those bumpy bus rides through the Jersey countryside, with the windows open and the spring air pouring in, they must have found each other and forgotten about me.

I had no idea, not a clue about any of this until an early evening in the end of spring. Crossing campus after a late baseball game, I saw my best friend and my best girl come giggling out of an empty building. The air got punched right out of me as I staggered behind a tree and watched them disappear into the twilight.

Nearly as painful as that torturous moment was watching Todd and Brenda fall for each other. Over the last few weeks of school, they became the pets of campus, and if we had a prom they'd have been the king and queen. As it was, everyone just fawned with approval as they pawed each other in public. It made me sick. The thought of what they might be doing out of public was too much for me to even think about.

Knuckling some salt into my gaping wound was the fact that neither of them said a word about this whole relationship. Not a word. Brenda and I were officially "only friends," but great friends, all year. And it was more than that, too. We spent a ton of time together, and chemicals, or something, bounced back and forth when we were alone. I was funny with her like nobody else, and she had a special smile just for me. I'd never been in love before, but I knew when it was happening to me.

And I knew when it wasn't happening anymore, too. Brenda and I stopped hanging around alone together. And she stopped smiling at me like she had before. We had conversations, I guess, about things, but nothing important. Like normal friends, I guess. Todd, on the other hand, disappeared altogether. Spring was busy, with sports and everything, and we only had a few weeks left before summer, but he never came to our floor in the dorm and, when he saw me around campus, he'd just go the other way or walk right past. He'd walk right past with this smirk on his face. I swear.

So another school year ended with me lonely and let down. And another summer was spent at home in Queens, mostly in my room, hoping for better days to come my way in the next year of high school. My last year. My last year and my last chance to make all those things I dreamed about real. They would come, and they would hurt, and it would all be worth it.

The Domino Effect

Chapter 1

The tree line whizzed past. Pop played a jazz station and tapped out a tune on the steering wheel. My mother had given me a thousand kisses before we got in the car. She also mauled my cheeks with giant pinches. She couldn't make the trip because of some big case she was working on, and she must have felt bad and took it out on my poor face. I felt bad, too, beyond the face job, because it left me alone with Pop for a couple of hours — me, staring out the window… him tapping out jazz on the steering wheel.

We hadn't spoken since the George Washington Bridge, when we picked up the highway that cut across Jersey. We hadn't spoken, but Pop looked over at me about a hundred and fifty times. I slouched down in the front seat of our fancy sedan and kept my eyes out the window, wondering about what waited for me at Hamden Academy.

The summer had been long but not in the good way. Our house was quiet, with my mother working lunatic hours as a new lawyer, and Pop and me still without much to say to each other. He did his thing. I did mine, which was going back and forth to a summer job at a supermarket and, at home, sitting in my room listening to Springsteen records and reading comic books. Good

Andrew Cotto

times.

But what I did mostly, besides work and sit in my room, was worry. I worried about what was going to happen when I got back to school. Todd Brooks and I had agreed to be roommates in one of the fourth year dorms, but that was before all that end of the year business with Brenda, him stealing my girl and never saying a word about it. Just thinking about Todd Brooks brought the taste of dirty pennies to my mouth. And I was thinking about him hard as we made our way across Jersey.

"Hey," Pop said. "You going to wear that face the whole way?"

He had on old jeans and sandals and a button-down short-sleeve shirt. In a lot of ways, being a musician and all, he still seemed young; but he seemed old and wise, too.

"What face?" I asked.

He took his eyes from the highway and looked at me. "That *funji-face*," he said. "You had it on since we crossed the bridge, makes me think that something's wrong." He gave me a wink.

Pop was a great winker. I swear. He used to do it all the time to me growing up, always at the right time, too, to make me feel better about something or other. I got over his winks as I got older and not so nice, but they still made me feel good, even though I didn't let on.

"Nothing's wrong, Pop," I said.

"You sure?" he asked. "Because from where I'm sitting, it seems like something might be wrong."

Pop's not a tall guy, really, kind of stocky with big forearms, while I'm taller than him and skinny, like my mother. But Pop always seemed tall, especially when he talked serious to me and, at that moment, he seemed especially tall with me scrunched down so low in the seat I was practically on the floor. So I sat up straight and looked out the windshield.

"Keep your eyes on the road, Pop."

He turned down the radio.

"My eyes are on you and on the road," he said. "No matter what I'm doing, my eyes are on you."

"That's nice," I said, rolling my eyes.

"Hey," he said, taking my forearm in his strong grip. He could bend pipes with those things, I swear. "Hey," he said, again. He liked to repeat himself like that, to make sure he had my attention, especially when I was being a smart mouth. "It's my job to make sure you're alright. You're my son. Not some kid I put food in and clothes on and share a roof with. Or some kid that I drive back and forth to sleep-away school. You're my son. My son..."

"You said that already," I interrupted, again with the smart mouth, but he kept on as if I hadn't said or done anything rude.

"...and you mean more to me than anything, anything, and it's my job to make sure that you're OK, and that you're growing up into a solid young man. A young man your mother and I can be proud of and send out into the world. *Capisci?*"

I used to answer him back in Italian when I was a little kid, but I didn't do that anymore.

"Got it, Pop," I said, starting to slide down in my seat again.

"You know, I could help you, Pal. I could help you with what's bothering you."

"Nothing's bothering me," I insisted, without too much patience.

"OK," he said. "Be that way. But know this, alright? Know this. I'm worried about you, and I think we're running out of time. I was against this whole sleep-away school thing..."

"It's not sleep-away school, Pop. It's boarding school," I interrupted, but he kept on as if I hadn't said or done anything rude.

"...and that was your mother's idea and I fought her on it, I'm telling you I did, but she got her way, and that's how it goes sometimes, but I'm telling you this, I want to see some maturity coming out of you this year. I want to see that kid your mother and I spent a lot of time raising. I want to see that kid become the young man we know you can be. I know you've had some hard times. I know it and you know it, but you gotta get over those things or they'll eat you up. *Capisci?*"

"OK, Pop," I said in a way that made it clear I wasn't taking him all that seriously.

We drove along in silence for a minute, and I could feel his eyes on me.

"So?" he asked.

"So, what?"

"You going to tell me what's wrong or what?"

I actually thought about it for a second. I swear. Growing up, he'd helped me, plenty of times, sort things out in the neighborhood with my friends and whatnot. So I knew, way down, if I told him the whole story about Todd Brooks and Brenda Divine, he would have some solid advice or something for me, some way for me to deal with the problem waiting in my room. But I didn't know where to start. Talking about what happened last year, and talking about it with Pop, of all people, seemed too hard. So I didn't say anything. But I didn't say anything rude, at least, either. I just sat there with my eyes out the window, watching the tree line whiz past and worrying about what was going to happen when I got to Hamden Academy.

———

We arrived as the campus was coming alive. Students and

their parents lugged suitcases and trunks and whatnot in and out of the dorms. We drove through the area with the main buildings, under the Arch and around a field where the girls played hockey, to a parking lot between the two dorms where the fourth year men lived.

I knew my dorm and room number already from a letter I got over the summer, so Pop and I started to carry in my stuff and stack it on the landing, next to my door, on the second floor. No sign of Todd Brooks yet, and I thought, for some reason, it meant something good that I got there first.

With only a few trips to the car left, Pop disappeared. No sight of him until I brought everything else inside. He came out of the stairwell, wrapped an arm around my shoulder, and nearly cracked my collar bone with a short, hard squeeze.

"Take care of yourself, Pal."

"You going already?"

"Yeah," he said, nodding and looking around. "Seems like you got things under control here."

"Where you been?"

"Me?" he asked. "Nowhere, really. Just taking a look around."

"How'd that go?"

"Not bad," he said. "Place seems safe."

"Good to know."

"Yeah," he said. "Well, OK, Pal. Take care of yourself. You'll call home every Sunday, right? And you'll behave yourself, right? And you'll look out for other kids and do what's right, right?"

I nodded to all his demands, not really paying much attention until he walked through the doors. And when he was gone, I went upstairs to check in and get the key to my room.

"Say that again?" I begged the guy who ran the dorm.

He'd just told me something that nearly knocked me over. This guy was turning into my favorite guy, fast. When I'd gotten there, just a minute before, he'd called me by my name, Daniel, even though I'd never met him. I figured he maybe knew who I was because we'd had a big baseball season last year, and I'd been the best guy on the team, and they gave me an award at dinner one night, so maybe he remembered me from that or something, though he didn't look too into sports, being middle-aged and kind of dorky. He wore glasses. I think he coached the drama team or something. Either way, I was pretty flattered and everything that he knew my name, but more happy about something else he'd said to me, so I asked him to tell me again what he'd told me before.

"Pardon?" he asked, having a hard time keeping up with all that I was thinking and the little I was saying.

"What you said before, about my roommate," I said slowly.

"Oh, yes," he caught on. "I'd assumed you would have known this already, but apparently your roommate, Mr. Brooks, will not be returning to Hamden Academy."

It sounded even better the second time.

I thought about asking him to tell me again, I swear, but instead I had mercy on the guy and signed something on a clipboard, took a key to my single room and got right out of there. Going down the stairs, I squeezed the key in my palm and tried not to trip, though I could barely feel my feet.

Even in all that excitement, I still noticed, on the floor in the stairwell, a milk crate full of trophies and stuff, with a big pair of ugly wrestling shoes on top. They were tied together, bright blue with some sparkled gold writing on the sides. I tried not to notice, but I did. There was something about them that couldn't be ignored.

Alone in my room for a couple of hours, I unpacked, stuck some posters on the wall, and set up my desk in the back by the window. I stood over the CD player when someone knocked on my door.

"It's open."

In came Sammie Soifer, smiling like a goon.

"Hi, Danny!" he called, catching his shoe on the linoleum as he crossed the room. I took a step to meet him and grabbed his hand. The poor kid's palm, moist and sticky as a raw meatball, reminded me of when I met him the first day of school last year. He'd been my roommate and the first friend I'd made in a while. He was nice as hell to me, all year. I should have treated him better. Everybody should have.

"What do you say, Sammie?" I asked. "How you been? How was summer?"

"Great," he said, rubbing the back of his arm, up and down. "Great."

"You in this dorm?" I asked him.

"Yeah," he said, kind of shy. "Right next door."

"That's cool," I said. "That's cool."

He sort of smiled in a relieved kind of way.

I returned to the CD player on the trunk between the two desks. "You're just in time for some Springsteen."

His sneaker squeaked again. "We better not, Danny," he said from the hallway. "We'll be late for the meeting."

"Relax," I said. "What are we gonna miss anyway?"

"You never know," he said. "It's… it's some crowd."

Sammie seemed nervous. He was always a little nervous, but he seemed especially uptight just then. I'll never forget his face when I told him we wouldn't be rooming together for fourth year. The little color he had went right out of him. Unlike me, though, he knew how to forgive. At least, that's what I thought at the time.

"Alright, alright," I said. I put the CD away and joined him outside my door. I peeked over the wooden railing at the group gathered for our first dorm meeting. A few new faces along with the many whose names I'd forgotten over the summer. It's not that I wasn't a friendly guy or anything; it's just that I wasn't good with names. Or faces. I used to be. I swear.

Sammie and I shuffled down the stairs and entered through swinging double doors. In the common area, sunlight flooded the checkerboard floors and white cinder block walls. Sammie joined the guys in back who hadn't arrived early enough to grab a seat in the lounge area or on one of the small couches dragged over from the lobby. I walked up to a black kid I'd never seen before, hogging one of the frayed Naugahyde jobs in the last row.

"You mind?" I asked, pointing to the space where another body could fit.

"*Jccht*," he hitched with his mouth, sort of sucking his teeth, like he was either calling a horse or really pissed off about something. I stood there, waiting for a horse to show up or for him to move over. He moved over, not too fast and with a groan. *Friendly kid*, I thought as I looked toward the front of the room.

Up there stood Mr. Good News from upstairs, – a tubby thirty-something in a bright sweater and black-rimmed glasses. He cleared his throat a couple times until the blabber died down.

"Welcome gentlemen," he said. "This is Montgomery Hall, for fourth year men at Hamden Academy. If you're in the wrong dorm, or the wrong school for that matter, now is the time to confess."

He spoke like he was on stage, but we stared back at him as if the blank TV screen behind his head was more interesting. It might have been.

"Well, kudos then," he offered, clearing a hunk of rust-colored hair that had fallen over his glasses. "For those who might have forgotten since check-in, I am Mr. Wright, a literature teacher here at Hamden Academy, the director of the Drama Club and, of course, the dorm master of Montgomery Hall."

The kid next to me called another horse, "*Jccht,*" but no one seemed to notice.

After a rundown of the many dos and many more don'ts, we were asked by Mr. Wright for some information about ourselves, including where we were from. Most of the 30 or so kids were from somewhere New (England, Jersey, York), with others spread out around the East Coast, Pennsylvania, and even into Ohio. There were some spots of color in the room from Asia, the Middle East, and the guy next to me (from some hostile land, wherever that was), but it was, for the most part, a white-bread crowd, though we didn't look quite like the perfect kids in the pamphlets handed out by the admissions office.

I guess a mixed student body is what you get at a pretty new private school that's been named after its town, rather than after some loaded dead guy who started the school back before electricity. The second-class status was alright by me, because it was still a good school, but it also had room for refugees.

"I'm Danny Rorro from Queens," I said to the room when it was my turn to speak. "One thing I like to do is play baseball, and something that makes me unique is that I think this whole grunge-rock thing is a fad."

I'd said that last thing strictly for Meeks and Grohl, who were into those bands out of Seattle and other soggy places. I heard Meeks groan as I turned to the stranger on my right.

"Terence King from Houston," is all he said. He didn't even bother standing up. I guess he didn't have anything that made him unique, except for the fact that he was the only black dude in the room (the school, actually, but he might not have known that, yet); or that he somehow managed to effectively conceal the eight-foot pole up his ass; or even the fact that he came all the way to the northwestern corner of New Jersey from Texas. Man. Texas. That seemed farther than China.

At Hamden, you didn't see a lot of kids from the South. I don't know why but, if I had to guess, it'd be the food. Straight Yankee grub. Beef and potatoes in six rotating forms: stewed, boiled, loafed / mashed, baked, twice-baked. Occasionally, they threw a roasted chicken out there or some WASP version of lasagna homemade by the Stouffer's Corporation.

"Not exactly an inspiring performance," Mr. Wright said, rubbing his trimmed brown beard after everyone was finished. I don't think he was eyeballing anybody in the room for the lead in this year's drama production. "But it will have to do and, unless there are any questions, we can all be on our merry…"

Everyone started to get up.

"I got something to say," Trent McCoy blurted.

Everyone sat back down.

"Well, by all means." Mr. Wright granted him the floor with a theatrical hand gesture. "We have an open floor policy here at Montgomery Hall."

A yellow-haired slab of meat lumbered up front and he didn't have to clear his throat to get our attention. They brought this McCoy gorilla in last year to make sure we kept winning National Wrestling Championships. The school had this huge reputation for wrestling, which was good, I guess, if you're into that kind of thing, but bad because it was the only thing we were good at, so knuckleheads like McCoy ran around like they owned the joint, which they kind of did. I'd seen him, of course. You couldn't miss the kid, always with this look on his face like he just ate something awful (probably the potatoes), but I'd never heard him speak until then, and I thought a few words might change my impression.

"One of ya' stole my shoes, and I want em' back."

I'd liked him better before. In the dead silence, a couple of people coughed. Someone, Meeks probably, whistled through his teeth, but it couldn't cut the tension caused by someone stealing from a wrestler. Why rich kids steal, I had no clue, but for whatever reason, things disappeared all the time in the dorm. I knew this personally. But this was different. Much different. Nobody messed with the wrestlers. They were students, technically, but wrestlers really, and, because of that, they had a separate standing or something. They even had their own dorm (or used to), and their own table in the dining hall. Going to their games or matches, or whatever they called them, seemed mandatory, though they never really talked to anybody else. Like I said, nobody messed with them.

"Ah, excuse me," Mr. Wright interrupted with every adjustable part of his face moving upward. "You believe someone stole your shoes?"

I bet Mr. Wright there was already regretting that open floor policy.

"Wrestling shoes — I won Nationals in them last year," McCoy barked, somehow thickening his already thick neck. "They got stuff written on the side."

"Yeah," puny Jeff Chester jumped up to get his buddy's back. This kid had come to Hamden from the same hometown in Ohio as McCoy. He wrestled smaller guys. Much smaller. Him I'd heard speak, plenty of times, in class where he asked more questions than a game show host. It wasn't like he had anything to say, or was even interested in the subject. He was just one of those kids who had to hear his own voice as often as possible. I sat as far away from him as possible, and never ever looked at him outside of class. Now he was living in my dorm, standing in front of the room, and getting ready to do even more talking in his Ohioan twang. Super.

"We was taking a break from moving our things upstairs and left them over in that stairwell there for just, like, 20 minutes before they was gone."

I didn't know what they were feeding those kids in Ohio, but it definitely wasn't brain food.

"Hold on now." Mr. Wright stepped toward the two wrestlers with his hands up. "Are you absolutely certain?"

"Yeah," McCoy confirmed, while Chester looked around the room for signs of guilt. Now this was funny, because the kid was, like, 5-and-half-feet, tops, and he couldn't have weighed more than my mother, but people were actually intimidated by the little loudmouth, just because he was on the wrestling team. Heads started dropping all over the place.

Mr. Wright jumped on the opportunity to act like a teacher. "I see. I see," he said. "These shoes, in the literary tradition, are more than just shoes. They're symbols. They mean more than what they represent in the literal sense. They are trophies. Like the white whale in Moby Dick, or Daisy in Gatsby, or..." He continued to run through his list of symbols, but nobody listened. Heads stayed down as Chester continued his scan.

After what I'd been through back home, I wasn't about to be scared by a pip-squeak with a cold stare, no matter who he hung around with so, when his eyes met mine, I shot him a wink and motioned with my head for him to move on. He didn't smile or anything, just looked to my right and locked his eyes on the new black kid. Now this was interesting. I didn't think anyone would say anything out loud about skin color being a big deal or anything, but even more tension entered the room as Chester stared at the only black face in the crowd. Terence King from Houston just sat there, though, staring at his sneakers, messing with his fingernails. Chester crossed his arms and waited. What a tool, that Chester.

Mr. Wright finally stopped his symbolism lecture, and the silence was worse than his words. I swear. A real shift spread throughout the room; you could feel it, like in the movies when nothing is really happening on the screen, but the music changes and the tension builds and builds and builds until you can't stand it anymore because you know something is about to go down. Terence King from Houston must have felt it, too (about time). He picked up his head and looked around. All the eyes darted away until he came to Chester, who held his gaze.

"The hell you looking at?" Terence King asked.

"Wha-whad'you say?" Chester stammered back.

"You heard me," Terence said, sitting up.

With proper posture, this guy, Terence, was even taller than he'd seemed all slouched on the couch.

"Oh no, no, no!" Mr. Wright insisted, stepping in front of Chester with both hands up like a traffic cop. "No, no, no!" he said again. Some authority figure. He should have gone back to his lecture on symbolism and bored us into a coma.

Big Boy McCoy side-stepped Mr. No-No-No and bore his eyes down on Terence.

Terence twisted up his face and glared back at McCoy. "Oh, you want some of this?" he asked, rising beside me on his long legs. This all happened fast. Too fast. Sitting right next to Terence, I could feel his energy start to snowball. His hands flexed, his nostrils flared for air, and his shoulders jerked. He, for the first time, checked out all the strange faces in the room. He must have felt very alone.

There was a hint of body odor from the jolt of adrenalin that swirls in the moments before a fight. McCoy studied Terence for a second, then stepped toward him. The room practically burst into flames.

Like most everybody else, I hated fights. They were one of the worst things in the world. Your heart throbs and bloods rushes your brain, and your mouth goes dry in an instant, and you can't find your breath no matter how hard you try, and all you want, all you want in the world, is to be anywhere but where you are right then, standing there with your body bailing out and your brain cursing you for ever having fooled yourself into believing that fighting was a good idea. But unlike most everybody else, I knew, no matter how it seemed at the moment, a fight wasn't the end of the world. You survived either way, and you lost either way, and hopefully you were able to avoid such situations in the future by minding your own business, which was my new motto: Mind Your Own Business. And even though I was in the perfect position to help, I sat back and watched. And what I saw was pretty amazing.

Nobody knew what to do. Bodies bumped into each other trying to get out of the way, or separate the guys anxious to fight. Couch legs squealed across the waxy floors, and you could hear people moan and gasp because they wanted to run away but had nowhere to go. Poor Sammie backpedaled into the corner and hugged himself like he was next on McCoy's hit list.

Tiny Chester tried to sneak around the crowd, but was held down by a few guys smart enough to keep busy with a safe and easy job. A group by us, on the couches in back, stood up and kept Terence from going anywhere as he jabbed a finger and shouted threats over their heads. McCoy, no master of language, passed on the verbal part of the program and moved around the common area furniture. He plowed through the crowd, and it seemed certain he was going to get to Terence and was only a few scared separators away when Mr. Wright — in possibly the boldest move ever attempted in the history of literature/drama teachers — removed his glasses, stepped onto a couch, and leaped through the air onto McCoy's massive back. I swear.

McCoy staggered forward but didn't fall, then shrugged Mr. Wright to the floor, bringing everything to a halt. Everyone circled around poor Mr. Wright, who was on the ground and not moving. It was a heavy few seconds, thinking about an adult being hurt, and the reality of reporting to the headmaster that our dorm master had been knocked cold during the first meeting of the year. Great start. But Mr. Wright moved, and everybody began to breathe again. Once on his feet, he pulled his sweater over his exposed belly and, with wild eyes, ordered, "Everyone to their rooms until dinner!"

Cool with me, I thought. *Time for some tunes.*

Chapter 2

From the second story window of my single room, I could see most of campus. The small field in front was empty. The skirt-wearing hockey players, with their wooden sticks, must have climbed up the hill beyond the other sideline and returned to their dorms. Being the first day of school, everyone had to be back for a 4:00 orientation. I figured the other meetings had probably gone better than ours had.

To the right of the field, an asphalt path split the backside of campus and sloped up toward the main buildings. The stone, ivy-covered monster in the middle spread across the ridge. Our dining hall was on the first floor, and the younger girls slept upstairs below the slanted roof that shimmered in the afternoon sun.

A patch of trees, just past the field, blocked from view the glass corridor that connected the dining hall to the administrative wing, where more ivy climbed over more stone to where even more girls slept upstairs. The other end of the administration building neighbored the unofficial center of campus — the Arch — which appropriately arched in brick over the campus's only road before connecting to the mail room. Below the mail room was The Canteen, the only place on campus to get a decent bite to eat.

To the right of The Can, and closer to home, I could see the white spire of the Chapel just past the roof of the old Victorian that housed the fourth-year women. Even closer was the back of the gymnasium complex, divided into brick and cement compartments. And right next to Montgomery, off the bend in the path, was the other dorm for fourth-year guys, Carlyle House, an identical rectangle of cinder block, glass, and not a bit of charm, built back in the '70s when Hamden Academy (thankfully) went coed.

There was more to the campus, like the academic building opposite The Can, and the new Language Arts building across the field to the left of Montgomery. Beyond sight from my window were the old wooden dorms over the hill, where the younger kids lived. I was glad not to be in those dorms anymore. I was a fourth-year student, on the back side of the school grounds, living all alone in a dynamite room that looked over the campus like I owned it.

I turned from the window when the music began, called by the notes of an electric guitar going 'round and 'round and 'round. Then an organ hummed and drums joined in with a boom-roll-crash! A saxophone smoothed out the melody: *ba-da-vum–voom, ba-da-vum–voom, ba-da-vum–voom, ba-da-vum—voom...*

I shot across the floor with the opening verse of "Rosalita (Come out Tonight)." It had been awhile since I'd jammed along with my favorite Springsteen song, but the news about my backstabbing roommate not being at school was reason enough to try and coax old Rosie out of her room. I rocked out in front of the closet mirror in nothing but black bikini briefs. A push-up routine, picked up over the summer, had given some shape to my shoulders and chest, but I was still pretty much a noodle with nipples, to tell the truth.

I raked a hand through my black hair, letting it separate in the middle and layer into place, over the top and down the back where it hid my thick scar. My head had been busted in Queens, and my heart torn apart at Hamden last year, but I raised my fist and imagined myself a rock star on stage. I got chills thinking about all those people cheering for me, but I'd pretty much given up on being adored by the crowd. All I needed to save my last year as a high school kid was a couple of solid friends and someone to love. And touch. All over. That's all. Everyone else could leave me alone. My fourth year had started off pretty good: no friend-turned-enemy in my room, solid Sammie next door, Meeks and Grohl on the first floor. Best of all, I had a someone to love. My Brenda Divine was across campus by now, I figured, safely in her room in the Victorian dorm.

The only problem on my plate was getting a tie fastened by 6:00. Dinner at Hamden Academy was a mandatory, semi-formal affair and, even after a year's practice, I couldn't get the knots just right without trying 10 times. So, while dancing around in my undies, I strung the first tie around my neck and worked a knot while The Boss and I continued to woo Rosie with promises of skipping school, playing pool, and being cool... staying out all night.

My tie was in place for the best part of the song, when the whole band, together as one, claps and yells about Rosie's papa thinking that I'm no good. I danced on the mattress of my no-show nemesis in tie-bouncing near-nakedness, back in front of the make-believe crowd as the energy built and the big news got dropped on Rosie's old man. Two lines into the song's final frenzy, I whirled to find a real-life audience standing in the doorway: Dorm Master Mr. Wright and Terence King from Houston.

"Hello, Daniel," Mr. Wright droned over the blaring music. He had a hand on his hip and a face with no patience. "Sorry to interrupt your little performance, but I've been knocking for ages." I stayed on top of the bed, still rocking a little from both momentum and shame.

It wasn't too often that I was speechless, but being busted in nothing but a paisley necktie and eye-patch underwear had my tongue tied. I stepped from the mattress, walked across the room, put an end to the music, and returned with my wits.

"What's with the pants?" I asked, with my hands out to the side.

Mr. Wright shook his head and entered with the stone-faced boy from Texas. I motioned for them to sit on the bare bed while I scrambled into some dinner clothes. Then I faced them from the opposite bunk, all of us with elbows on our knees, positioned for a serious discussion.

"Now, Daniel," Mr. Wright began after adjusting his glasses and taking a giant breath. "As you are aware, we had an unfortunate incident at our meeting today, involving Mr. King here and the two other boys."

"Mr. King" had his eyes on the floor. He had round cheeks, puffy like ravioli, but a sharp, clenched jaw. He scratched and matted the tight waves on his head. He had on some untied white high-tops, oversized designer jeans, and one of those short-sleeved alligator shirts.

"Danny," I said, sticking out my hand.

"Terence," he responded with a deep voice, his long arm reaching mine across the open floor. He pushed out his purple lips and squinted before turning his eyes down and away.

"Well," Mr. Wright continued, "it's my responsibility to oversee such matters, and considering no blows were actually exchanged, or even attempted, I've decided *not* to report this matter as a fight *per se*, but only as inappropriate behavior."

"What's that mean?" I asked.

"It means that the potential pugilists won't have to face the headmaster with the possibility of expulsion, but instead must accept the punishment as determined by me — two weeks of Sunrises."

"Ohhh!" I reared back, thinking of those clever-named but brutal 6 a.m. detention session. "At least it ain't February," I said to Terence.

He gave me about half a second of eye contact before turning away.

"Of course," Mr. Wright continued, "this leniency comes with promises from each to refrain from any subsequent confrontations. Isn't that right, Mr. King?"

"Yep," he answered, then took a turn studying the white-paneled ceiling with cheap tube lighting.

"We all know the consequences will be dire if there is such an event," Mr. Wright said, with all the authority a tired, flabby English/drama teacher could drum up. "And considering all three are scholarship students here, I feel it would be best to keep them as separate as possible to avoid any embarrassment for the school, as well."

"You got a scholarship?" I asked Terence.

He smirked. I was impressed (with the scholarship, not the smirk). I turned back to Mr. Wright, thinking of the usual so-called students who hogged all the scholarships.

"What are those guys doing here anyway?" I asked.

"Pardon me?"

"Those guys. The wrestlers. What are they doing here?" I asked with raised palms. "I thought they had their own dorm or something."

"The floor in the underclass dorm, previously allocated for the wrestling team, is being utilized to accommodate a significant increase in the student body."

"Hey, good for Hamden," I said with a shrug.

"Yes," Mr. Wright agreed. "The headmaster is very pleased."

"Too bad for us," I added with a wink. I was a pretty good winker, too.

"Truly," he agreed under his breath.

"You ever think about joining up with those guys?" I asked Mr. Wright. "That was some move you pulled down there."

Now both of my guests had the straight face going.

"OK, OK, I get it," I said. "So you want Terry to move in here-"

"Terence," Terry said.

"What?"

"Name's Terence," he said, a note lower on bass.

"Whatever you want," I agreed before turning back to Mr. Wright. "So you want Terence here to move in with me to be on a different floor than the guys upstairs."

"Bravo," Mr. Wright said, with his own brand of sarcasm. *Not bad.*

"What about the other singles?" I protested. "I know Sammie, right next door, has a single, too."

"Well, with you being the star of the basketball team-"

"Nah, nah, nah," I interrupted. "I'm not the star of the basketball team! I bite at basketball. You must be thinking of baseball. It's baseball I'm good at. That's how you knew who I was, right? Because we had a good season last year and they gave me that award at dinner and everything. Remember?"

His flat face convinced me he wasn't searching through any memory files. "You were on the basketball team last year, correct?" he asked mechanically.

"Yeah, but only because I had to do two sports. Not this year. No way."

"Are you making this intentionally difficult for me, Daniel?"

"I don't know. Maybe a little but I'm also setting the record straight."

"Consider it an arrow," he said, standing to signal the end of our discussion.

"One more thing there, Mr. Wright…"

"What's that, Daniel?"

"Danny," I said. "I go by Danny, and I'm wondering who else this has been unfortunate for?"

"Pardon?"

"You said before that 'we' had an unfortunate incident, and I'm wondering who this has been unfortunate for besides me and him?" I flashed Terence one of my winks, but he didn't seem all that impressed. Tough crowd.

"*Juh swee tro fat-e-gay*," Mr. Wright moaned on his way out.

Once he hit the stairwell, I turned to Terence and poked my thumb toward the door.

"Did he just say he was fat and gay?" I asked.

"*Fatigue*," he said with the appropriate accent, "means tired in French."

"I was gonna say," I shrugged.

With fists jammed into his pockets, Terence strolled over to the window. "It's that bullshit about *overseeing* I got a problem with. That and him being the dorm *master.*"

"Say that again?"

"Never mind," he said, repeating the "*Jccth*" sound he seemed so crazy about. On a trunk between the desks sat my small CD player. Terence poked a button and the lid flew open.

"So, ah," I asked, reminded of my recent embarrassment, "you into Springsteen or what?"

"Nope," he said and stared out the window.

Pebbles bounced off the glass. Terence stepped back and faced me.

"Oh, those are my guys," I said. "You going to dinner? You can come with us, but you gotta get dressed first."

He didn't say anything, so I asked him again if he was going to dinner.

"Nope," he said, turning to look over the posters hung all over the room: Bruce in concert from the early days, a NY Met here, a NY Met there, Christy Turlington for inspiration (now useless, thanks to Mr. 'I'm not going to report this as a fight, *per se*').

"Alright then," I said, grabbing my dinner jacket. "I guess I'll catch you later."

My new roommate said nothing.

This is going to be some year, I thought on my way downstairs. Too bad I wouldn't see the end of it.

—

"And what else happened?" Meeks demanded as I walked to dinner with him and Grohl and Sammie, who had caught up to us on the path.

"Nothing!" I said to the freckled bag of bones who was already on my nerves. "I told you already," I said, leaving out the part about being caught dancing in my undies "they showed up, we had our little chat, and then he told me he doesn't like Springsteen." I poked Grohl on the shoulder of his leather blazer. "Can you believe that? Doesn't like Springsteen?"

"It's, like, the '90s, man," Grohl said. "Why don't you listen to somebody else?"

"I don't like anybody else."

He scoffed, patted the top of his mousse-piled hair, and

checked the status of the shack. The smoking shack, a piece-of-crap Peg-Board shed, sagged beneath a weeping willow across the field from Montgomery. Kids could go there and smoke or just hang out, and there was usually a decent crowd during off-hours from studying and whatnot.

"And that's it? That's all Terence or Terry had to say?" Meeks asked.

"Oh, yeah — he had some problem with Mr. Wright saying *oversee* or something."

"The hell for?" Meeks asked.

He was full of questions, that kid.

"I think it's a racial thing," Sammie said. "You know, like the guy who looked after the slaves was the overseer, I think." "Hey, Sammie," I said, "thanks for the history lesson, but you heard the man. It's, like, the '90s, alright? The 1990s. Don't give me any noise about slavery."

Poor Sam. Even when he was right, which was practically all the time, it ended up, somehow, like he was wrong.

"Wow, that's pretty amazing," Meeks waxed sarcastic as we crossed the road and entered the courtyard between the two main buildings. "It's his first day at a new school and the guy tries to take on the Wonder Twins. You'd think he might have more to say about it."

"What can I tell you?" I asked, putting on my jacket in the reflection of the corridor that connected the structures. "Anyway, I'm the one who should have something to say about it. I had to give up my single room." *And moments alone with Christy Turlington!*

"Never mind," he said, passing into the marbled walkway. "Serves you right anyway."

I spun him around, and he looked at me with more guts than

a kid of his size and upbringing should have. Meeks was a preppy derelict who'd been booted off to boarding school from his rich Jersey suburb.

"Say that again," I challenged, not all that excited about taking crap from a guy wearing a green jacket with a pink tie.

"Relax," he backed off, in his usual way. "I'm just saying."

"Just saying what?"

"I'm just saying," he continued, his strawberry hair under my eyes, "we have two blockbuster stories on the very first day of school, both of them running right through your room, and you don't care about either of them."

"What do you want from me?" I asked him.

"First," he said, counting with his finger, "the shoes. Did your roommate steal them?"

"What?" I asked, shocked. "Nobody took those things."

"Earth to Danny boy. In case you missed it, we got a shoe thief in the dorm."

"Says who? Chester and what's-his-face McCoy? That moron probably left them things back in Palookaville, OK? I mean, come on, things disappear. I know it firsthand. Remember my lucky shirt from last year?"

No one seemed to remember me searching the dorm, over and over last spring, for a T-shirt of mine that had vanished. It was just a crappy shirt, given to me by a beautiful girl named Brenda Divine. It had meant a lot, but only to me. "We're talking about valuables missing," I continued. "Not used wrestling shoes. What kind of weirdo would take those things?"

I don't know, Danny," Grohl chimed in, still looking around as he talked. "Both Chester and McCoy seemed sure they were in the stairway and, you know, based on how your roommate bugged out, he looks like the prime suspect."

"Suspect?" I asked. "What are you guys, the freaking Hardy Boys all of a sudden?"

"Just ask him about the shoes, OK?" Meeks said.

"Yeah, OK," I cracked. "I'll get right on that one, Geoff."

"Good," he said, as if I was serious. "Second, what happened with Todd?"

I expected that question, and had no answer, but was kind of curious myself. I mean, what could have kept that kid away? I was thinking (hoping) a shark attack off the coast of Martha's Vineyard, or maybe some sort of alien abduction where they probed all his holes with painful things.

"I can't help you there, either, Geoff," I said. "I don't know about Todd."

Sammie and Grohl tugged their ties and watched people enter the dining hall.

"Geez, Rorro," Meeks blurted. "What good are you? You didn't know your roommate wasn't coming back? You didn't even talk to him over the summer?"

"Why didn't you talk to him?" I shot back at Meeks. "You've known him longer than I have."

"I was in Ireland all summer," he said, like it was no big deal.

"Yeah, well," I said. "I was in Chinatown." I'd stocked shelves all summer, in a Chinese market in Flushing.

"It doesn't matter where you were," he said. "You're supposed to talk to your roommate. It's code. I called this dope from a pub in Dublin." He smacked his roommate on the arm, and Grohl nodded like it was law.

"Yeah, well, good for you, but after what that guy did to me, what'd you want me to do? Call him up to see how far he's getting with Brenda? And maybe, while I'm at it, find out what side of the room he wants?"

Meeks rolled his eyes and looked at me all disappointed. "Danny, Danny," he said with fake pity. "She wasn't your girlfriend."

"Close enough," I said.

"And besides," he said all matter-of-fact, "there are no rules for chasing the cat."

"Oh, OK," I said, shaking my head, baffled by some of the so-called rules these morons had. "Whatever you say. But if you want to find out why he ain't here, Sherlock, you can go ahead and call him yourself."

"I already left him a message," he said. "I'll let you know what he says."

"Do that," I answered, my voice echoing in the hall.

"Ah, we better get in there," Sammie pointed out. "We'll be late."

"Only if this guy's done breaking my shoes," I said.

The boarding school guys loved the expressions from back home, and I tossed them out whenever I was in a jam or needed a laugh. Sammie and Grohl laughed at my shoe-breaking line, but Meeks managed to keep his face straight.

I pointed at my shoes. "Done with them already?"

"I am," Meeks said, releasing his smile. "For now."

"Super," I muttered as we approached the dining hall, and the first rib-sticking meal of the year.

"Hey," I said to Meeks at the smoking shack afterward. "Thanks for telling me dinner was optional. There were three people at my table."

Seating was assigned for lunch and dinner, even when you didn't have to be there.

"Dinner was optional," Meeks said, as he scanned the decent crowd that surrounded the rotting shed.

"You're a real pal," I said, kicking lightly at the dirt.

"It was our first chance to check out some of the new *Bettys*. Besides, would you have rather stayed in your room, talking about nothing with your new roommate?"

"Good one," I said. "Got a smoke?"

"Ask him." He nodded at Grohl, who was busy with some younger girls.

A couple dozen people milled around, but I didn't bother with them. I bummed a smoke from Grohl and returned to Meeks.

"He starting already?" I asked.

"No rest for the wicked," Meeks said, flipping that scary green jacket over his shoulder.

"So why ain't you mixing it up?" I asked.

"Got nothing to say," he spat like a child. "Thanks to you."

Not good-looking or talented or anything, Meeks got by mostly on information. Gossip was his game. That and a smart mouth, but the smart mouth usually came after he got to know you through gossip. He knew about most things going on around campus, and used that information to get to know people, especially girls. I couldn't believe some of the girls he ran around with. Foxes. I swear. Out by the shack that night, I started to feel sorry for poor Meeks with nothing to say. People were talking about the fight, and the witnesses from our dorm were all holding court in separate circles. Meeks told good stories, and he could have stolen the show, but he didn't deal in known information, and the fight, at that point, was known.

"Hey," I said to Meeks. "You know he got an athletic scholarship, right?"

Meeks perked up. "Who?"

"Terence King from Houston."

"Get out of here," he said. "For what sport?"

"Field hockey," I joked.

"Basketball?" he assumed. "They gave this guy a basketball scholarship to the World Wrestling Academy? Are you sure? Are you absolutely, no-doubt-about-it sure?"

I nodded.

"Hey, hey people," Meeks called, walking into the crowd. "Get a load of this..."

I went in the other direction, toward the edge of the smoking area. I dropped the half-finished butt and rubbed it out with my shoe. Those things tasted like death, and that funky Styrofoam feeling in my mouth always reminded me of that day at home when I busted those windows and choked down half a pack of my mother's smokes. I spit on the ground and waited for my Brenda Divine to walk by.

I stood there alone as the sun went down. A cool, kind of pink twilight hung above the hills that rolled off into the distance. After the hills disappeared into darkness, I kicked around with a small group of guys I didn't really know. After talk of Terence and the fight had finally finished, and most people had gone back to their dorms, I listened to what I hoped were made-up stories of summer girls and summer places I'd never know.

The walk home across the field was quick, but the lobby and common area were dark by then. All the couches had been straightened, the TV screen was back up on its perch, and there was no noise from the laundry room or the pay phone around the corner. You'd never be abe to tell that a serious brawl — including wrestlers, a basketball player, and a high-flying English/drama guy — had nearly broken out there a few hours earlier.

Upstairs in room # 7, Terence was behind his desk in saggy

shorts and a basketball jersey. His bed was made and a few things, mostly books, were neat on the shelf.

"How's it going?" I asked.

"*Aight*," he said, not lifting his head from a book.

"You didn't miss anything at dinner," I said rolling up the posters, which had been taken down from his side of the room and left on my bed. "You didn't even have to be there, being the first night and everything."

"I know."

How come no one told me?

"Well," I said, after tucking the posters away, "you got any questions or anything?"

"No."

"I don't think you have to worry about them guys," I said, sitting on the edge of my bed to slip off my dress shoes. "They're stupid, but not, you know, retarded or anything."

"I'm not worried," he said, holding my gaze.

"Alright," I said. "Good for you."

I swapped my dinner clothes for jeans and a T-shirt. I didn't feel funny getting changed for the first time in front of a stranger, since he'd already seen me dancing in my underwear. I brushed and flushed in the bathroom down the hall, and when I got back, Mr. Wright stood in the open doorway.

"I'm glad to find you decent this time," he said, with this devious kind of smile.

"Yeah," I said, sneaking by him. "Me, too."

"But you're supposed to be in the room before check-in, Daniel, not during."

"Yeah, sorry about that," I said, putting my toiletries away in the corner closet.

"Well, I'll let it go this time."

I thanked him and sat on my bed with my back against the shelf and my feet over the edge of the mattress.

Mr. Wright took a few steps into the room and crossed his arms as he looked to the desk by the window where Terence sat.

"So," he began. "Now that everyone has had a chance to settle down, can I assume this matter is behind us?"

"Ask them," Terence spat, his face twisted up like a pretzel.

"I will be asking them as well, young man, but now I'm asking you. I trust everyone involved will honor their promise to be on their best behavior from now on."

"Mm-hmm," Terence mumbled. He clamped his hands behind his head.

"Very good," Mr. Wright said, relaxing his arms down. "And things are going well in here, also?"

"Mm-hmm," Terence repeated.

"And for you, Daniel?"

"You mean besides the fact I can't shut this guy up?" I said, mocking a gabbing mouth with my hand.

Mr. Wright let out a little gust of air. "Well, it's been a long day for all of us," he said, "and I'm sure tomorrow will bring better things."

*About time…*I thought, desperate for all those things I'd been denied.

Chapter 3

On the first day of school, I went to classes, ate a meal, and looked all over for Brenda Divine. After seeing the same faces too many times, I started to worry that she wasn't coming back, that she and Todd had run away together. I pictured him pulling up in front of her house in a sports car or something, and driving away together with the windows down and the radio playing. Then I started thinking that I'd listened to too many Springsteen songs. Still, I started breathing easier when I spotted Brenda underneath the Arch.

"Bella Faccia!" I called to her. Her arms were tanned under a dress with no sleeves. Her cheeks looked a little emptier than I remembered, but she was still the most beautiful person I'd ever seen.

"*Bella Faccia*," she echoed with half-a-smile. "I haven't heard that in a while."

"Where you been?" I asked playfully. "I've been looking all over for you."

"I was looking for you, too."

"Really?" I said, straightening my spine. "How come?"

"Nothing. Well, something," she said. "I have to get going, but I want to talk to you about Todd."

"What about him?"

"He didn't come back, did he?"

"No," I said.

She exhaled. Kids shuffled by with their backpacks and whatnot, but Brenda seemed to be staring at the ground, off in space or something. She raised her head and her eyes didn't seem as green as I remembered. A sparkle or something was missing.

"What?" I asked. "You didn't know?"

"Not really," she frowned. "We sort of broke up."

"Say that again?"

She did, and I nodded even though I felt like breaking into an embarrassing dance.

"Well, I want to talk to you about that," she said, moving toward the academic building. "Can you come by after classes tomorrow?"

"Why not today? I'm good today, you know. Today... works."

Very smooth.

Brenda blushed at my enthusiasm. "I have to talk to the soccer coach today," she said. "I'm not playing this year."

I should have known right then that something was wrong, because Brenda not playing soccer was like me not playing baseball, and I could never even imagine that. But at the time, all I *could* imagine was me and her meeting after school the next day.

"What time?" I asked.

"After classes," she said, for the second time.

"Sure thing," I said. "After classes." I suddenly had a shirt full of spiders, though I fought the urge to wiggle until she walked away. Then I wiggled and filled up like a helium balloon.

Instead of floating off to class, I walked a couple of loops through the Arch, then ducked into the mail room. I was the only one in there. There were two walls lined with fake-gold boxes, and a long wooden counter where bigger packages could be retrieved. You could also purchase school supplies, and just about any other item you wanted stamped with the name of Hamden Academy in bold.

The last wall was all cork, and covered in tacked notices I never read because they only listed stupid things about clubs or dances or whatnot. During the wrestling season, the boards held nothing but fliers about their matches. But this day was different, because it wasn't even close to wrestling season, yet they'd taken it over already. The only thing up there — all over every inch of the boards — was a WANTED poster, with a photocopied picture of some wrestling shoes. On the bottom, it read: Dead or Alive. It didn't make sense, of course, but the message was clear. At least it was clear to me. I should have known Mr. Wright was nuts to think that the deal with the wrestlers was going to go away just by moving Terence downstairs. I'd seen this kind of thing before.

The next day, right after last class, I walked under the Arch, over the road, and across a grassy meadow to the old wooden mansion where the fourth-year women lived. The brown paint peeled in some places, but the house stood in pretty good shape. A stoop led to a wraparound porch and a screen door. I wiped my palms on my dress pants as Brenda came down the wide staircase of the open foyer. She had changed into old jeans and a gray Hamden T-shirt. Her hair bounced in a ponytail.

"Hello," she said businesslike. "Ready to go?"

"Sure," I said, hurrying to get the door for her.

We walked away from her dorm on a path around the grass. Instead of handcuffing herself to me in a flurry of regrets and apologies, she brought up what was already an old subject of the new school year.

"So, um, have you spoken to Todd yet?" she asked.

"Nah," I answered as we passed the chapel. "Meeks is trying to get ahold of him."

"You didn't talk to him *at all* over the summer?"

"Nope," I said, as we followed the limestone stairs down to the basement of the academic building.

In an empty classroom, she sat at a front row desk as I hopped up onto the large teacher's unit. We sat silently for a minute, her eyes on the shaded hill that sloped toward the campus gates, my legs flopping as I thought of something clever to say.

"I know he's going to be missed around here," Brenda declared, still staring out the window.

"Yeah," I admitted. "He was the mayor, alright."

She kept her eyes away from mine and tucked a strand of hair behind her ear. "Have you heard anything about *why* he didn't come back?" she turned suddenly to ask.

"No," I said, kicking the desk with my heels. "Why do you care so much, anyway?"

"What?"

"I thought you guys broke up?"

"We did," she insisted.

"Get over it then." I didn't mean to say that, or say it like that, at least, but it came out cruel anyway.

"I am. I mean, I'm try..." she fumbled a little before her face curled up like she'd just sucked on a lemon. "I'm just wondering if people knew why he wasn't coming back, OK?"

"OK," I said, kind of calm, but then that strange tone came back. "What's everybody asking me for anyway? What am I, his spokesman or something?"

"He was supposed to be your roommate, wasn't he?" she asked. "And your friend."

"He was supposed to be my roommate. That's true," I said, crossing my arms. "But he's no friend of mine."

"What are you talking about, Danny?"

I couldn't stand the way she looked at me, like I wasn't special or anything to her, like she hadn't been dying to see me the way I'd been dying to see her. She just wanted information from me, information about somebody else. It hurt so much.

"Come on, Bren," I said, trying to prove my importance. "You of all people should know why that guy is no friend of mine."

"How long has this been going on?" she asked.

"What?"

"Your animosity toward Todd?"

"Animosity?" I said. "SATs are over, alright? Give it a rest."

"I'm serious," she persisted. "Have you been mad this whole time?"

"I'm not mad," I said, with a face and an attitude that must have proved me a liar. "I'm just not interested in being friends with some guy that steals my girl, that's all."

"Your girl?" she repeated. "Your girl? I'm not a possession, you know."

"Really? You should have told that to Todd."

She shot to her feet. "Why?" she asked. "What did he tell you? What did he say?"

I could see her coming apart, her eyes and ears and lips kind of moving in different directions. But I spoke anyway, thinking more about my pain than hers.

"He didn't tell me anything," I said defensively. "I'm just saying you should have told Todd you weren't a possession before he wore you around like a hat last year."

"I can't believe you just said that," she said.

I couldn't believe it either. What a prince. Brenda began to tremble, then she ran from the room with tears falling down her beautiful face.

That went well.

—

I gave Brenda time to clear before climbing the stairs that left me outside The Can. Through the window, I saw Meeks and Grohl at our regular booth in the far corner with a few girls I didn't know. A short line waited to order at the counter. Smoke rose from the grill. Upstairs, the Foosball table was open. I jingled the pocketful of quarters I had brought with me and turned for home.

I was damaged — OK, *stupid* — enough to hurt someone I cared about and still feel like the victim. I went back to the paranoid — OK, *stupid* — idea I'd held onto since things went bad for me back home: the world had it out for me, simple as that. What a dope.

I was making a sad march home to the dorm, rubbing my scar and feeling sorry for myself, head down and eyes on the path, when a wrecking ball knocked me to the ground. Spun halfway around, I sat up without breath, clutching my throbbing shoulder. Up the path, little Chester patted big McCoy's back as they continued on their way, laughing hysterically.

Super.

I didn't feel like getting up. Nothing inside me wanted to fight gravity or anything else. Right there on the ground, flat on my ass, holding my shoulder, seemed like a good place to be. But then I figured that, at some point, somebody would come along and I'd have to tell them what I was doing there on the ground, flat on my ass, holding my shoulder. I didn't want to bother with that, so I stood up, dusted off, and went on home. I walked into the dorm and straight up the stairs, thinking that at least no one had seen me out there on the ground. I was ready for the quiet of my room.

"You alright, man?" Terence asked as soon as I entered. He was standing behind his desk with his eyes all bugged out.

"What?"

"I saw that shit, man," he said, pointing out the window. "That was messed up."

Some day I was having.

"Yeah," I mumbled, yanking off my dirty pants. "What are you gonna do, right?"

"I don't know," he said, with raised brows. "You could punch one of them hillbillies in the eye."

"Yeah, I guess," I said, "but guys like me don't get off easy," I said. "And I ain't going back to Catholic School for nothing."

"So you just take that from them?" he asked.

"I've had worse."

He raised his head and eyeballed me. "Oh, so it sucks to be you, huh?" he asked.

"There you go," I said with a wink.

I changed my pants, sat down behind my desk, and looked out the window. It seemed like the best place to be.

Chapter 4

Terence was a room jockey. He spent his free time in our second floor hideaway, riding his chair. I joined him (in my own chair, that is). While the other students did their thing in the warm September weather, Terence kept his head in a book, and I looked out over campus hoping to spot Brenda strolling down the path on some sort of mercenary mission to save me. I knew I was nuts, but still I kept watch.

One afternoon, a couple of buffoons exited Carlyle and made for Montgomery. A minute later, as expected, someone knocked on our door. I ignored it.

"Yo, yo, anybody in *dere*?" a voice crooned.

I cursed under my breath as I crossed the room to open the door.

"Rice!" I cried. "Where the hell you been?"

"What?" the long, pale figure in the doorway asked.

"A real, live black guy in our class, and you're just coming by now?"

"Oh, that's funny, that's funny," he nodded. "But we here now, ain't we?"

"Yeah, too bad," I said and motioned him in with my head, but he didn't move. He just stood there with his hand perched out to the side. I didn't go for the fancy handshake game. Can't two guys just shake hands without making a show out of it? I let Rice hang there for a bit, with his hand held out all ridiculous like that. Then I eventually, offered him my hand, which he grabbed and groped and squeezed through a couple of poses.

Rice was really William Miller, a moron, wrapped in a riddle, wrapped in an Air Jordan sweat suit. He thought he was black, so people called him Rice as a reminder of what he was as white as. He lived in the other dorm, Carlyle, where I wished he still was, instead of *poppin'& breakin'* into our room with his stoner sidekick in tow.

Rice waddled toward Terence like some sort of ghetto penguin. "Bill," he said, and swung a handshake from the hip. "I'm your power forward, G," he said.

Terence looked stunned.

"This here's my boy, Santos," Rice said, with a thumb dunked back over his shoulder. The pudgy heir to a Puerto Rican rum dynasty stood with his back to the closet and his hands clasped in front of his crotch. His eyes were glassy, and he reeked of weed. He nodded at Terence, and then at me. Santos and that goon McCoy could have had some conversation — nothing but nods and grunts.

Rice helped himself to a seat on my bed, crossing his long legs. "We heard about your all *sitch-eation'* and shit with them man-huggers," he said to Terence. "They talking about it all over school and shit, don't *cha* know."

"Who is?" I asked.

"Everybody, G," he said. "And you know them wrestlers is feeling it, too, 'cause of them signs and shit they put up in the mail room."

"What signs?" Terence asked. "Where?"

"Ah, don't worry about it," I said. "It's nothing."

"Oh, yeah," Rice said to me with his chin up. "And I heard

them fools put a big hit on you and shit out there in broad daylight and shit."

Super.

"Stop saying that, *and shit*, every time you open your mouth, alright?" I said. "That was an accident out there. They don't know me from Adam."

"*Sheet*," Rice tried to drawl. "You *trippin,*' Home Slice. This shit's on, for real and shit, like it or not, and shit. We got a player now, took one of their scholarships, too." He turned to Terence and asked quietly, "You got a scholarship to come here, right?"

Terence nodded.

"Solid!" Rice cried, and smacked his hands together. "Who hooked you up? Carolina? Georgetown? Duke Blue Devils?"

"Ah, Brown," Terence said, fingering the pages of his book.

"Brown?" Rice asked, recoiling. "They got a squad?"

Terence leaned back in his chair and crossed his arms. "Lost to Princeton last year in the Ivy League Championship," he said. "The same Princeton that beat Georgetown in the first round of the NCAAs."

"Alright, then. Alright, then," Rice said, standing up, his stringy hair bouncing above his eyes and over his ears. He began to pace the small space between the beds, talking out loud to no one in particular. "We good. We good. And once we have a season, man, one good season, this school's going to be about basketball. Basketball. Not that Greco-homo-erotica stuff they doing on them mattresses and shit."

Santos, with his back still to the closet, nodded as his partner continued. "It's on alright, and that business with the shoes, and this guy here, this hero, standing up to them, just set it off early. That's all."

"Relax, Willy," I said. "Nothing's happening."

"I don't know about all that," he said, rapping his knuckles against his chest, "and when it goes down, y'all just *holla'*." He jerked a thumb toward the neighboring dorm. "We got *cho'* back."

"OK, then" I said, rapping my knuckles, then pointing toward the door. "Got it."

He stood up, and smoothed out his sweat suit. "In the meantime, y'all just let us know when you ready to run some ball and shit."

"We'll keep it in mind," I said. "And shit."

"Do *'dat*," he said before easing toward the door. "Later y'all." Santos nodded and followed his friend out.

After they left, Terence and I resumed our positions of study. I couldn't help it. I swear. I had to look at him. He looked right back at me. We turned our eyes toward the open doorway that Rice and Santos had just exited. I tightened my mouth to keep from laughing. It was hard.

"The hell *was* that?" Terence asked, his face puckered.

I started to answer, but a howling came from my throat. Terence smacked his desk and tried to hold back a smile. We traded glances and then just started to crack up. A minute later, we were laughing like lunatics, right there at our desks, practically falling to the floor.

When we stopped laughing, Terence straightened his face and raised his chin. "You sure there's nothing to worry about with those wrestlers?"

"Nah," I said, trying to seem certain. "Nothing at all."

I'd been having trouble sleeping, thinking about Rice and everything he said about the wrestlers and their signs. So, after hours one night, I slipped out of the room and down the stairs.

Quietly, I entered the corner room. In the dim light, a figure, low to the ground, reclined below the arch of headphones. On the far side of the room, between the desktops stacked with jewel boxes, Grohl sat on the window's ledge and fingered his guitar in the silvery moonlight. Upon spotting me, he raised his head. I held a finger to my lips as I crept up slowly behind Meeks, pulled the big ear cushions back and released them into place with a snap.

"Ahhhh!" he screamed, flopping from his bean bag chair and onto the floor.

"What are you listening to there, Geoff?" I asked casually.

"You dick!" he squealed.

"Relax there, chief," I advised. "You'll get us busted."

He made a bulldog face and started to get himself together.

Murky sounds leaked from the headphones, and I picked up the CD booklet to look at the Pearl Jam artwork. "Maybe if you listened to some respectable rock-n-roll instead of all this gloom stuff you wouldn't be so edgy."

"Bite me," he said, wrapping the cord around his headphones.

"And what's with the flannel?" I asked, flicking the booklet. "They look like the Brawny Paper Towel band."

"So, what's up?" he asked. "I thought you only left your cube for classes and dinner these days?"

He had me there. I really had been spending a lot of time in my room. It was nice and quiet up there with Terence. And a little bit lonely, too, to tell the truth.

"Yeah, well, I'm curious about all this noise with the wrestlers," I said. "Rice came by last week talking a lot of smack."

"Rice," Meeks laughed. "He must be touching himself over this."

I confirmed that fact, then asked if there was anything to it, or if Rice was just being a basket case like always.

"You really should get out of the room sometime, mister," Meeks said. "Someone yanked down their posters in the mail room, and now all of them, not just McCoy and Chester, are more pissed than ever. There're even a couple of new goons they got that are extra special scary." I'd seen them — a square, dark-haired kid who seemed old enough to be somebody's uncle, and a tall, hyper guy with a buzz cut that made him look like a walking boner. Still, I had my doubts.

"Come on. What? Over some shoes? And some posters?" I asked. "No way."

Meeks rubbed his hands together and spread his lips into a wide grin. "The working theory out there is that the school's looking to transition from wrestling to more mainstream sports, and Terence, with his scholarship, is just the first step. They say the headmaster asked him to stay up in his room to, you know, not jeopardize anything."

"Aw, come on, kid," I laughed without thinking anything was all that funny. "That's *fagakada* and you know it. The headmaster didn't ask anybody to stay in their room."

He laughed at my *fagakada* line then told me again that that's what "they" were saying.

"Oh yeah?" I asked. "And who's 'they'?"

"Rice," the roommates said at the same time.

I ran a hand through my hair.

Grohl stopped noodling around with his guitar. "If you think about it there, Dan," he said with a too-cool tone, "it makes a lot of sense."

"No, *John*," I said. "If *you'd* think about it, it makes no sense at all."

The roommates shrugged in sync, like they'd lived together

too long. They had.

"I'm out of here," I said.

Meeks called me back. "You probably didn't hear about Pride Day either... ?"

Pride Day was this ridiculous weekend when we play our rival — The York School — in every available sport to make up for the fact that we didn't have a football team. Alumni and parents came, and everyone yucked it up and pretended they were all best friends for the day. At night there was a bonfire out on the fields. I hadn't mentioned it to my parents, second year running.

"What about it?" I asked Meeks.

"Todd's coming." He jetted his brows, up and down. "Maybe we can put the band back together and have some giggles... that is, if you're done crying over that Betty."

I wasn't.

"No chance," I said. "But thanks for the info."

In bed that night, across the room from a steadily breathing Terence, I decided that the best way for him to squash the rumors would be to get out of the room and show his face around campus, even if it meant hanging out with Rice.

—

I felt a little naked there in the gym, wearing standard-issue athletic shorts from my old Catholic school. They were regular gym shorts, with piping down the side and around the top of the leg. Terence, Rice, and Santos had on these droopy drawers that looked like pajama bottoms. They busted my chops the whole way to the gym, but I thought they were the ones who looked ridiculous, especially Santos, whose shorts nearly touched the back of his hundred dollar high-tops.

"*Aight,*" Rice said after we warmed up. "Me and Santos

against you two fools, two out of three, up to 11, bring it back to the foul line, winners keep, losers pay for Birds afterward."

The Early Bird was the best breakfast sandwich on the planet, the Canteen's masterpiece of bacon, egg, and cheese on grilled sourdough dripping with butter. I took Rice's challenge, right away, without even checking with Terence.

"Check," Terence said, bouncing the ball to Rice, who returned it and crouched into what he must have considered a serious defensive pose. Terence snapped a pass over to me on the side of the key, and I waited as he trotted down to the baseline. I had about a foot on Santos, and held the ball over his head until Terence had pushed his back up against Rice. He called for the ball. "Give it up. Give it up." No problem. Terence caught it with a clap, sending a smacking sound through the gym. After a head and shoulders fake, Terence wheeled around the bean pole, bounced the ball once on his way to the rim, and rolled it in like he was playing by himself.

I laughed. "This ain't gonna take long."

An hour later we were at The Can, sitting in a booth with four Early Birds, four Cokes, and a basket of fries. We'd killed those guys, mostly because of Terence's face-job on Rice, but I'd helped, too. And let me say, for the record, that there ain't a short, fat, pot-smoking Puerto Rican on the planet that can guard me one-on-one. If the league was full of guys like Santos, I might have gone out for the team again, but as it was, I was happy just to do my part in having some fun and earning a free meal.

"You know," I said, slowly separating two halves of the sandwich, allowing a string of orange cheese to dangle like a telephone wire, "these things taste even better when they're free."

"Damn, dog," Rice moaned, crossing his arms and slumping into his side of the booth. "That's cold."

You could tell Rice was soft and spoiled by what a sore loser he was.

"You know what else?" I started again. "Based on that score, you should probably buy us another."

"What I *should* do," he spat, "is buy you some new shorts and shit."

"Hey, these things are lucky," I said, rubbing my short-shorts.

Terence and Santos laughed at the back and forth between me and Rice.

"I'm sorry you ever brought this fool out," Rice sulked to me about Terence. "How'd you change his mind anyway?"

"I told him I knew how to get the only good meal around," I answered, elbowing Terence. "On the biggest *fool* around."

"That's cold, man," Rice whimpered. "That's cold."

"Yeah, you said that already, *dawg*."

I nudged Terence again, then looked over at Santos. He had a sweet smile on his fat brown face. I shot him a wink and he nodded. Poor Rice seemed to be the only one not having a good time. "Hey," I said to him. "What's with the *funji* face? So you had to buy some Birds. But now you know that scholarship wasn't wasted on a stiff."

"Yeah, you right," Rice said, correcting his posture. "Solid!" He slapped Terence five across the table.

We polished off the food while Terence checked out the hokey decorations and the wooden tabletops left empty by those (somehow) not interested in wrecking their appetite for dinner. The upstairs game room had a few students watching the giant screen TV in their dress clothes. A young couple played Foosball. Ouch.

On the way out, I got stuck holding the door for a group of girls I didn't know, except for Brenda Divine, who was bringing up the rear. She had on this swinging skirt that kind of danced above her knees as she walked. Her sunshiny hair rested on the shoulders of a button-up sweater. My normal blast of adrenalin upon seeing her was cranked even more by the flowers I could smell when she stopped in front of me.

I'd been trying to make eye contact with Brenda for weeks, after I figured the smoke had cleared from our little exchange. She hadn't looked my way, not even once, and I'd all but given up on Brenda Divine... or at least I'd begun the process of trying to get started on thinking about giving up on Brenda Divine. But now she stood in The Can, right in front of my face, reaching out with the same silence and sad eyes she'd had that lousy day in the classroom. Even in my state of constant delusion, I sensed she was giving me a chance. And I wasn't going to blow it.

"What's the matter, Cinderella?" I asked. "Bluebirds don't make your bed anymore?"

"No, they don't," she said with a banged-up smile. "They haven't for awhile."

"Sorry about that," I told her. Then I told her again.

"Me, too," she said, squeezing my wrist before walking away.

"Hey Bren," I called after her. She turned around in the middle of The Can. "You think these shorts are, you know, too short?" She gave me the once-over and then covered her mouth as she cracked up laughing.

Chapter 5

I liked sports and everything, and I loved playing baseball, but I didn't buy any of that "Big Game" business, like it was the end of the world if Hamden Academy didn't beat the York School every time we faced off in some competition. Without a football team to pile our hopes on, the other fall sports — soccer, field hockey, cross-country — combined to take on this special importance during the second Saturday in October. What made this whole deal even funnier was that York's rival wasn't even Hamden, but some school called Milton. They played each other in football on the first Saturday in October.

Hype ruled all week, with banners covering campus and announcements every night at dinner. The worst part was that the players took it all seriously, and they walked around like big shots all week (like the wrestlers did all year), even though they were mostly missing the two things needed to be good at sports: strength and skill, which the wrestlers, unfortunately, had by the bucketful.

Anyway, I wanted no part of Pride Day, especially since Meeks had been blowing his horn all week about Todd coming back. This was worse than the hype for the games. The thought of Todd being around bothered me, since I didn't know how I'd react. What do you do with a guy like that? Someone who hurts you on purpose even though he's your friend? Do I forget it, like Meeks and Grohl suggested, since all *is* fair when it comes to girls? Or do I go batty on him until I feel better? I leaned toward going batty, so I decided to make myself scarce on Pride Day.

My favorite part of the Hamden campus was the Far Fields recreation area. Starting on the front side of the gym, and extending out behind our dorms, was this enormous collection of fields. We had separate sections for everything: soccer, lacrosse, softball, baseball. I almost fell over my first time out there. I'd never seen so much grass in my life!

In the spring, there could be four games going on at once, but the only fall sport out there was soccer, men's and women's, side by side, on the first two fields (field hockey was in front of Montgomery, and cross-country took place somewhere in the country, I guess). The baseball field angled away from the woods in the far corner, and that's where I went with my pride on Pride Day.

After sleeping in, kicking around, and having a late lunch alone, I left the crowded campus and walked behind Montgomery onto a wide trail through the woods. Once out on the open fields, the bonfire contraption was to my left, dead center in the middle of the expanse. I hugged the right side of the woods, walking away from the soccer games in the panhandle above the gymnasium.

After reaching the baseball diamond and walking behind the pitcher's mound, I was pretty much out of sight. I lay down in the grass. With hands behind my head, I looked up at the blue, blue sky. Not a cloud anywhere near New Jersey that day.

Lying there, alone and out of sight, a slight breeze swept over surface of the earth. It swept over me, too. The bent grass tickled my arms and neck. With the sunlight on my face, I closed my eyes and thought about things. I thought about my life and all the bad that had happened to me. I thought about the loss of

Genie Martini and my childhood friends in the neighborhood where everyone once knew me as Domino. I thought about that year at Catholic school, with its all-boys policy and its scary nuns. I thought about Todd Brooks and the fact that a crap kid like him got to be with a dynamite girl like Brenda Divine. And I thought about me some more. I lay in the grass feeling sorry for myself, wasting time while my last days of high school — my last chance at getting back all those things I'd lost — were whizzing past like trees on the side of the highway.

I opened my eyes. Overhead, two hawks dipped and dived in the swimming pool-blue sky. I wished I could swim. I wished I could fly. Tired of wishes, I hopped to my feet and ran across the field. I must have been laying there for awhile because, in the distance, the soccer fields were empty. Some students and faculty stared at the unlit bonfire, and I booked it past them and entered the woods behind Montgomery. On the dirt path, I tripped on a root and tumbled over my shoulder, but I got up and kept going until entering Montgomery. I was going to shower, get dressed up nice, and spill my guts to Brenda Divine. After I apologized, about 10 times, for making her cry.

Cutting through the common area, toward a shower and some sharp clothes, I heard a little bit of noise — laughter, voices, music — coming from the corner room. I stopped. I should have kept walking, but I stopped without thinking and knocked on the door.

"Who is it?" a voice called out.

"It's me," I barked over the music.

Waiting for the door to open, I tried to stay still, but my heart jumped like a small animal trapped in my chest, and breath

escaped from my nose in short bursts. My mouth went dry and
my hands got wet as I made fists for Todd Brooks. I was going to
walk in there and just kill him. I couldn't help myself. All I knew
about fighting, and all I had to lose by getting kicked out… all
those plans I'd had for Brenda were ditched the second I sensed the
presence of someone who had hurt me bad. I should have stayed
out on the fields.

After half a minute, I heard someone fussing by the door, and
then the lock popped and the door cracked open. Grohl pulled me
inside and re-set the lock. I searched the darkened room for Todd,
but all I found in the shadowy space was Rice and Santos, laid out
like lizards, stoned to the bone.

"What up, *Cuz*?" Rice asked, sprawled across a bed with his
legs hanging off. "We came looking for you *dawgs*, and found these
cats instead."

"Where's Todd?" I asked Meeks. He was sitting in his
beanbag chair with his hands behind his head, a surly look on his
pinched face.

"Didn't show," he snapped. "Thanks to you."

"Me?" I asked. "The hell you blaming me for?"

"Maybe if you'd just called the guy, told him you didn't care
about some stupid girl, he would've come."

"Listen up, ball bag," I said through my teeth. "I ain't your
social secretary."

Meeks tightened his eyes and duck-billed his lips. But he
didn't say anything.

In the background, the Allman Brothers Band played this
song with a winding guitar solo that had enough notes to fill a
Springsteen box set.

"Yo, yo," Rice waved his arms. "Let's squash that shit, *aight*?"

I kept staring at Meeks, and the little turd was doing a pretty good job holding my eyes. He had no idea how much anger he was messing with. I was thinking about walking over there and kicking him in the face, for starters.

"So where were you all day anyway?" Rice asked me.

"What?" I turned to ask.

"Where were you? We was looking for you before, and T said you might be down here."

"I went for a walk in the woods," I lied.

That was the first thing I could think of to say, and I thought it was better than admitting I'd been lying down on the ball field having a moment with myself. The room was silent for a few seconds before the three of them burst into hysterics. Maybe the truth would have been better.

"To the woods!" Rice cried. "What, like, on a hike? Nah, nah! I must be high! I must be high!"

"Looks like the woods won, Guy," Grohl said, slapping his thigh.

"What?"

"Looks like the woods won," he said, pointing at the dirt stains on the knees of my jeans and on the shoulder of my thermal undershirt.

"Hey, ah, maybe the next time you go out hiking, nature boy," Rice coughed, trying to contain his laughter, "you could get the Fresh Air Fund to go *wit chu*! Look out for your city ass and shit."

Santos, already on the floor, rolled over on his side and shuddered. All of them laughed at me, except for Meeks. He kept his little kid's pout, in his little kid's chair. I figured I'd better leave him there.

"Later," I said.

"Much!" Meeks's bratty voice chased me out the door.

The sky was stretched into faded blue when I burst out of the dorm. The tree tops had gone dark. Groups of students and parents funneled toward the dining hall, so I stomped across the field and into the smoking shack. No one was smoking on Pride Day, with parents all around, so I sat in the silence and the smell of rotting wood. I spat on the ground and cursed Meeks. I felt dirty and itchy in the dank room, but I didn't want to have to go back to the dorm for a shower and a fresh set of clothes. Another run-in with Meeks might cost me my night. Or more. I needed food and time to cool down, so I made a plan.

I wouldn't be allowed in the dining hall looking like one of the *Outsiders*, so I went to the Can to eat with the orphans. There were a dozen or so faces, either alone or in twos, none of whom I knew. I ate by myself. In the bathroom, I washed my face and neck and hands. To hide the stain on my shoulder, I inverted the shirt and made for outside.

I walked down the path and between the dorms, following the trail to the fields. The smell of wood smoke filled the air. The fire shot orange flames into the darkened sky. A good crowd had gathered, and I searched the glowing faces that surrounded the vigil. I didn't find Brenda, though.

I left the flames and followed the fields past the gymnasium complex. The back of Brenda's dorm was dark, except for a few glowing rooms. I thought about climbing up the fire escape, but figured I'd get in trouble, especially if I ended up knocking on the window of the wrong room, so I walked around to the front. The common area was empty, except for a bookworm-type girl reading under a library lamp. I took a deep breath and called on some courage, but none came. None came. I was out of guts. I sighed and walked off the porch, feeling kind of collapsed.

Chased by the noise from the headmaster's house, I cut across the meadow. On the path, I decided to skip the shack after seeing Meeks and them there, smoking their brains out. Loneliness seeped from my chest, hard and heavy, and I fought the urge to run while picking up my pace down the path. At the dorm, I entered the quiet lobby and, feeling numb and alone as I'd ever been, headed for my room.

"So," a soft voice startled me. "You finally made it."

Brenda Divine sat on a couch, a suede jacket laid over her lap, her hair fanned down to the shoulders of a black turtleneck.

I almost fell over.

"Come on," I said, helping her put on her jacket. "Let's get out of here."

—

We crossed the field and went up the hill and onto a gravel path, past the Language Arts building. After a rocky meadow with a crumbling cemetery in the corner, we hopped a low stone wall and caught a pitched trail through some open trees. The air smelled of earth and leaves. The sound of the crashing waterfall filled our ears before we reached the clearing that opened to an old wooden bridge spanning a falling stream. Brenda took my hand. We walked.

"I miss this place," she said as we settled on the bridge, our legs dangling between the rungs. The sky was hazy and blank, except for a harvest moon that hung above the trees.

"Yeah," I said, looking at the lights of the small town below. "It's some spot, alright."

I remembered how we used to sit on the bridge last year, talking for hours, sometimes not talking at all. And sometimes we would follow the stone steps alongside the waterfall, down to the empty lot that led to Main Street. We would kick around town and stop for lunch at the old diner before acting like little kids in the playground. I liked to push Brenda on the swings, touching the small of her back with my hands.

Once, just outside of town, I chased her through a field covered in dandelions. She laughed as I ran behind. After I caught her (and I'm pretty sure she let me), we stood still as agitated seeds floated around us like wispy fireflies. On the way home, she bought me a T-Shirt in the Five-n-Dime that read: wherethehellishamdenville? I treated that shirt like a trophy, until somebody stole it at the end of the year.

"I'm sorry, Danny," Brenda broke the silence, bringing me back to the bridge.

"About what?" I asked.

"I'm sorry about what happened last year," she said. The wind ruffled her bangs.

"Ah," I waved. "Forget it."

"No," she said. "I've been thinking about how hurt you were, and I can understand why."

"You can, huh?" I picked up a twig and began snapping it into pieces.

"Yes," she said, taking my arm. "I know that, at first, we liked each other, and flirted and whatever, but you knew I had a boyfriend, and I thought we became, you know, like real friends, and that made me so happy. I can't even tell you."

"You can tell me," I joked.

She poked me with her elbow and kept talking. "It was just that I never had any real guy friends because, every time I made one, it turned out they just, you know, wanted to be with me, and then there was you — this really cute, charming guy who was just happy to be my friend. It was so validating."

"There you go with them SAT words again, Bren."

"I'm serious," she said. "I know it seems, well, self-absorbed, but it meant a lot to me — though I guess I was wrong, and I'm sorry."

"First of all," I said, dropping the broken twig pieces into the pool below, where they circled, then shot away, "I prefer handsome to cute."

"Got it," she noted.

"And I did like just being friends with you; you were like my number one guy there for awhile."

"Thanks," she smiled, bumping my shoulder with hers. "I've never been anyone's number one guy before."

"Yeah, well, that's good, but I wanted more than that, too, you know. I wanted more than that." It felt weird to admit what I'd known for so long. My face grew tingly and my throat went dry.

"I know," she said, taking my hand. "I did, too, and I finally broke up with my boyfriend when I was home for Easter, and I was kind of giving myself some space and everything at first, and I didn't want to, like, you know, seem egotistical and make some grand announcement about it or anything, but I was going to say something to you. I promise, I was, but then Todd just came out of nowhere. And he came on so strong. He just overwhelmed me with notes and flowers and all this charm. I felt like a princess."

"I'm going to barf, Bren," I said. "I swear."

"No, no," she begged, taking back my hand. "I'll stop. I promise. But I want you to know that Todd told me he talked to you about us and everything. He told me he did and you said it was perfectly OK. He told me he talked to you."

I'm pretty sure my face said all I had to say about that.

"But he didn't talk to you, right?" she said, real sympathetic-like.

"Not a word, Bren," I said. "And I mean that, literally, for real."

"I'm so sorry," she said and held both my hands in hers. "I just kind of figured that out."

"Yeah, well, I'm sorry, too, Bren, that I made you cry like that. You didn't deserve that."

"No, I didn't," she said quietly.

Then she smiled kind of sad and put her head on my shoulder. Her hair smelled like my mother's fancy shampoo. We sat in the silence. I could feel my heart beating. My body tingled, and I felt super-charged and super-scared at the same time. I can't believe I was frightened, but I was somehow. I was. Fifteen minutes before that moment, I'd thought my life was crap, total crap, and now what I'd hoped for most of all, for so long, sat right next to me on a bridge, her hands in my lap and her head on my shoulder.

"Would you like to kiss me, Danny?" Brenda asked quietly, her words vibrating through my body.

"Yes!" I yelled, my voice echoing through the trees.

Brenda laughed and pulled back a bit. "Can we be friends again, too?" she asked. "I need you to be my friend again, too."

"Sure thing, Bella Faccia," I said. "Anything you want."

We kissed on the bridge. Her mouth felt warm and tasted like cream soda. Sitting there kissing, I didn't feel all that crazy energy like I used to with Genie Martini back in Queens. My body seemed as hollow and weightless as my dangling legs, and I was all of a sudden floored by the thought that maybe, just maybe, if you dreamed about something long enough, and hard enough, and often enough, it could actually come true.

Knocked out by wonder, I kissed and kissed with Brenda Divine, under the yellow moon and above the rushing water that circled and carried some of my pain away. Maybe some of hers, too.

Chapter 6

"I think we should find a better place to be alone," Brenda insisted as we came out a doorway into the afternoon light. It had been three weeks since we'd kissed on the bridge, and just as many secret places had been found by me and then rejected by her. My latest spot was a drippy hallway, connected to an abandoned locker room in a forgotten part of the gymnasium. Very romantic.

"I'm telling you," I said, "nobody comes in or out this way anymore."

We were on a little hill above the path, behind some bushes and still out of sight, though she acted, even under cover, like the whole school could see us.

"It's not that," she said, making sure the blouse she wore under my borrowed jean jacket wasn't too messy from all my tugging. "It's just we could stand a little more ambiance, don't you think?"

I skipped my SAT line. "It's practically winter," I observed, with an arm around her shoulder. "What do you want me to do?"

"Find a place that doesn't give me the heebie-jeebies," she said. We stopped on the path above the shack. She kissed me for incentive, but I was running out of ideas. Every time we got comfortable — and I had thought we were getting comfortable a few times — she would all of a sudden decide the place wasn't romantic enough or something. And I could barely even hold her hand in public. She didn't seem like the same girl who spent last spring on the lap of Todd Brooks. Still, I wasn't complaining, or giving up.

"How about the Chapel?" I asked.

"No way," she said. "I am not fooling around in a church."

"They're Presbyterians, for God's sake," I pleaded as she walked away. "What are they gonna do, report us to the *Catlics*?"

I watched her walk into the burning leaves of autumn, my faded jacket covering her narrow shoulders.

"Alright, alright," I yelled. "I'll work on it."

She stuck a finger in the air without turning around.

I laughed like a moron. I was happy about everything those days, and could feel this magic all over me. It was like having superpowers. But, to tell the truth, falling in love was better than having superpowers. It's better than everything.

On the path toward home, thinking about the next time I'd see Brenda (dinner: 70 minutes and counting), I saw a bunch of blue wool jackets with white leather sleeves outside Montgomery. The jackets were filled with sausages looking up at my window. Those guys — the sausages in blue and white casings — could easily have been waiting for me to go to dinner, if only it was an hour later and I'd actually had friends on the wrestling team.

"Why don't you come on down here?" Chester challenged the empty window as I arrived. "Are you chickens or what?"

Those two new goons were standing behind him on the grass, with their arms crossed. McCoy paced the path, punishing his palm with a heavy fist.

"Hey," Chester said to me as I tried to slip past. "Ain't that your room?"

Super.

"Yeah," I said. "So what?"

"Well, there's someone up there saying stuff to us."

"Like what?"

"Saying that we should get a room, like we're queers or something."

"Not in them jackets," I cracked.

"What?"

"Never mind," I said.

"Then they was laughing at us when we came over," he said toward my back.

I kept walking, but not fast enough. McCoy stepped in front of the door and crossed his arms. I was trapped: Blockhead in front of me / Blabbermouth behind. I chose the safer route.

"Listen up," I said, after turning to face Chester. "You must be confused, alright? Because that's my room there," I said, pointing to it, "and I'm standing right here." I pointed at the ground in front of me. "And my roommate, you know, the one I have because of you two numb-nuts," pointing first at Chester, then over my shoulder to McCoy, "is too smart to get mixed up in that rigamarole with you again. Got it?"

"What?" Chester asked, his face squirreled up with confusion. "*Rigama*...what?"

"I said there's nothing in that room that has anything to do with you or your stupid shoes, so give it a rest." I tried to walk away, but the barrel chest of McCoy stopped me.

I'd been bounced back a step, a big step, but I returned to where McCoy and I stared nose to nose, so close I knew he had baloney for lunch and some nostril hairs in need of a trim. I squinted to be tough, digging into his gray, gray eyes, but he didn't seem all that concerned. I figured he was deciding whether to eat me or kill me. We stared for 10 seconds that seemed more like an hour. When his eyes moved away, I felt relieved (and a little tough), but as soon as I breathed out, McCoy snorted like a rhino and shoved me over the table Chester had made on his knees behind me. I flew for a second, skidded for a bit, and ended up flat on my back on the path. Buttons of my plaid Polo shirt bounced in every direction. I had officially made their list. Super.

"I bet you didn't see that coming," Chester bragged over his shoulder as the group walked away, laughing. I thought about getting up and going after them, but I was tired of getting tossed around.

"One of you owes me a shirt," I yelled.

I brushed myself off and confirmed that the backside of my favorite khakis was torn, as if the gravel in my underwear hadn't already clued me in. I glared up at the empty window and stomped inside.

—

After taking the stairs two at a time, I ran into Sammie on the second floor landing, his jaw dropped and eyes bulging. He must have seen the whole thing out his window. He couldn't have been the only one.

"Whoa, Danny!" Stevie cried. "Are you alright?"

I brushed past him into my room. Terence, slouched across his bed, gave me a sheepish glance. No one else was in there. I sensed Sammie behind me in the doorway.

"Come out already," I said to the room, but nothing moved. "Get out here," I ordered.

Laughter blurted from Rice, Santos, Meeks, and Grohl as they emerged from their hiding spots — in the closet and under the desks — slapping each other five.

"The hell are you guys doing?" I asked, pissed off and embarrassed about getting dumped on my ass in public, for the second time.

"Just hanging out and shit, you know," Rice answered with a shrug.

"That's it, huh?" I challenged him. "Just hanging out?"

"Yeah, well, you know," he said, smiling kind of sideways. "We was up here *chillin'* when we saw them man-huggers walking past, and, you know, we couldn't help teasing them a little bit, that's all."

"Really?" I asked. "Couldn't help it?"

He made some sort of spastic gesture with his body that was supposed, I think, to represent a shrug. There was no talking to that kid. I ran some fingers through my hair, tried to calm down and be smart for a change.

"You should be careful with them guys," I said to the group before looking at Terence. "Especially you."

"Hey, man," he said. "I was just sitting here like this, minding my own business. I didn't say or do nothing."

"Yeah, relax, Dan the Man," Rice advised me. "It's cool."

"You call this cool, Bozo?" I ran a hand over my tattered pants and some pebbles tumbled out the bottom.

All of them, even Terence, laughed like hell. All of them except for Sammie. He looked kind of ill.

"You talk to them guys about this at all?" I asked him.

He shook his head.

"I thought you were tight with them."

"Nah," he mumbled. "Not really."

"What's the matter?" Meeks teased. "They didn't like the way you toweled off their balls last year?"

"Screw you," Sammie squealed. "That's not what the manager does!"

Sammie sucked at sports, and he got away with riding the bench for the soccer team in the fall, but he was sunk in winter and spring so, last year. he signed up as the equipment manager for the wrestling team. He even seemed like part of the team there for awhile. They'd given him one of their big, ugly jackets, which he'd worn all winter long. In the spring, after the season ended and I told him we'd no longer be roommates, he still stuck around those guys, even though they'd taken his jacket back.

"Yeah, well," I said to Sammie, "you're better off anyway." As for the others, I told them, again, to watch themselves and, most importantly, to leave me out of whatever they were doing.

"It's cool," I was assured, again. "It's cool."

It wouldn't be cool. For me most of all.

Before Thanksgiving break, there was a mandatory meeting for all fourth-year students. We trampled into the chapel and sat in the pews. The school's guidance counselor, a bald dude with a turtleneck under a corduroy jacket, spoke from the stage about college. We were supposed to be giving serious, serious consideration to the schools on our list, from long shots to safeties. There was some formula to be followed, a formula that had been outlined during previous, private meetings with him. I must have missed those.

I had no first choice. Or second. Or third. My safety, I guess, was St. John's University in Queens. Both my parents had gone there, and my father was pressing me, big time, to go there, too. He wanted me close to home, but all I knew about college was that it could, like boarding school, get me *away* from home.

The way it was laid out in the meeting, and in the conversations around campus, was that college wasn't something your parents decided. It was supposed to be our first big decision as adults and, if you got in, you got in. End of story. And even if Pop didn't think of me as ready for the world, I wanted out of Queens and out of his sight, and college was the way. I listened up as the counselor spoke of deadlines, and of all the brochures with applications still available in his office. I figured I better get moving soon, but I had better things to do first.

After the meeting, I waited on the edge of the meadow. Hats and scarves and heavy jackets covered the people sitting beneath the concrete sky. I dug my hands into the pockets of my thick leather jacket, but still, I shivered with anticipation.

"Hello, Daniel," Mr. Wright said, coming up beside me. Him, I wasn't anxious to see.

"Oh, hey Mr. Wright," I said, blinded for a second by his Technicolor sweater, paired with a bright red scarf. "How's it going?"

"Fine," he said, pinching his mouth to one side. "I was meaning to have you to my apartment, but I might as well speak with you now."

"No, no, it's OK, Mr. Wright. I'll come upstairs later. I'll come later. What time works for you?"

"I understand you were involved in an altercation, of sorts, outside the dorm recently." Not much of a listener, that guy. "And I wanted to let you know how troubled I was by that. Troubled and concerned."

"Hey. I was just on my way home, and those guys were messing with me. No big deal, though. Nothing happened."

"Well, I imagine there was more to it than that," he said, with that all-knowing tone adults have.

"Nah, not really," I said. "That was it."

He squinted and crossed his arms. "Despite my efforts, I suspect there is something going on, a rivalry of sorts, between the two camps, and I want it to stop."

"Talk to them," I said.

"To whom?"

"The wrestlers."

"I recently met with their coach, and it is his contention that his players are being provoked."

He was right, and he was wrong. Like a lot of things, it was kind of complicated. I probably could have provided some insight, some help in figuring things out before they got out of hand, but I didn't say a word.

"You know, Daniel," he said. "The reason I brought Mr. King down to your room is that I understood you were someone who could bring people together. An ambassador of sorts."

"Oh yeah?" I laughed. "Where'd you get that idea?"

"A little birdie told me."

"Nah," I said. "That's not me."

He stroked his beard and sized me up.

"Hey," Brenda, thankfully, interrupted

Within the gray surroundings her auburn hair seemed especially bright. She settled next to me, and it felt good having her by my side. With a mitten-covered hand inside my elbow, she shifted her eyes from me to Mr. Wright. I began to move us away, but she held me in place while extending her free hand. "Hi. I'm Brenda, Danny's friend."

"Hello Brenda," said the English teacher. "I don't believe we've had the pleasure. I'm Mr. Wright."

"Mr. Wright, huh?" She played her own straight man. "My mother said I'd meet you someday."

He laughed. She smiled. I pulled her along.

"Come on."

"OK," she said. "So long, Mr. Wright."

"*Au revoir*," he called after us. "Think about what I said, Daniel."

We escaped Mr. Technicolor Sweater and stopped on the road behind the dining hall, beneath a tree with bare branches. Dry leaves scratched past our feet as we kissed.

"What was that all about?" Brenda pulled away to ask.

"What?"

"What Mr. Wright asked you to think about."

"I forget," I said. "You ready to go?"

We'd been spending our afternoons in a classroom at the Language Arts building.

It was private and warm, and it only cost me a couple of Early Birds to get Grohl to cough up the information. I should have gone to him right away, because this place worked. I could feel Brenda becoming more and more relaxed, and I got to touch her and she touched me back. It's all I could think about. I tried to pull her along, on the road behind the dining hall, but she wouldn't budge that day.

"Was Mr. Wright talking about those boys?"

"What boys?"

"The wrestlers."

Brenda had heard about what happened. Everyone had heard. And even though I wasn't happy about it, I wasn't complaining either, because it was after she'd heard that things had started happening between us in the Language Arts building. I'd take that trade any day. Hell, they could have hung me from the chapel by my undies if it got me closer to Brenda. The bad thing was that she had gotten kind of obsessed with the whole rigamarole regarding the shoes and the wrestlers and my roommate, who still didn't talk to many people, or even come out of the room that much.

"I'm worried," she said. "Kyle Chester is in my math class, and he was talking this morning about what they did to you, and how they were going to find out who stole their shoes, *by any means necessary*. Those were his exact words. By any means necessary."

"Oh, boy," I laughed, and rolled my eyes. "Don't worry about those guys, Bren."

"I do worry," she said, taking my arm. "I just came from the mail room and they put those awful signs back up. This time in color."

"Wow," I cracked. "Color copies — what a time to be alive."

She smacked me on the arm and then balled the mittens on her hips. She looked so gorgeous and ripe I could have bitten her like a peach. I swear. "OK, you're right," I said. "Let's go to the LA building where it's safe. It can be, like, our hideout or something."

"Sorry," she said. "I'm busy this afternoon."

"Busy with what?"

"Well, that meeting about college really got me thinking about sending out a few more applications." She said it all perky and pleased with herself.

"I thought you were set on Connecticut," I said. She'd been talking about the University of Connecticut, her home state school, since we'd been together.

"I am," she insisted. "But a few more applications couldn't hurt."

I couldn't argue with that logic.

"And what about you, Mister?" she said, laying an open palm on my chest. "You haven't done any yet, far as I know."

"I know. I know," I said. "I will. I will."

"When?" she asked with some doubt. "Thanksgiving is next week, and that's the deadline for at least getting started, you know?"

"Hey, I was in there, too, Bren. I heard the guy."

"So… " She posed, with her hands on her hips again. "Come with me to the guidance office and pick up some applications or, at least, make an appointment with Mr. Dawkins."

"Who?"

"Mr. Dawkins," she said. "The guidance counselor, Danny, from the meeting you were just in." She didn't actually say 'duh,' but the way she spoke and the look on her face had 'duh' all over it.

"I'll go," I said. "I promise. Just not right now, 'cause I got something else to do."

"Fine," she said, and reached out to pinch my mouth together before walking away. She killed me, that Brenda.

I watched her go, her knees kind-of-knocking, and her butt kind of bouncing and her head held up high. She passed under the Arch and out of sight. Campus was quiet at this in-between hour of the afternoon, so nobody saw me follow Brenda toward the Arch, and nobody saw me slip into the empty mail room, where I tore down all those WANTED posters, just like I had before.

Chapter 7

I felt kind of jealous when the guys in the dorm talked of homecomings over Thanksgiving with their families, old friends, and local girls. The best I could hope for was to be left alone, for the most part, until it was time to go back to school. That was until I made a plan.

I took the bus from Hamdenville to the city and got to Queens late Wednesday night. We spent Thursday out in Long Island at my mother's cousin's house, where I shot baskets in their driveway most of the day, while her kids, younger than me, messed around on their rollerblades playing hockey. Mom was working Friday, and Pop had a football game at the high school he taught at in Brooklyn, with his marching band performing at halftime. He asked me to come with him about a hundred times, and I could tell he wasn't just being polite, but I had all day Friday set aside for a phone call.

"Hello," a man's voice answered. It sounded like he didn't like talking on the phone. I thought for a second about hanging up, trying again later in the day, but it had already taken me half an hour to get up the nerve to dial Brenda's number. The paper she'd written it on was getting crumpled and soggy. I hadn't called a girl on the phone since Genie Martini, the summer before 9th grade, and even then I'd tried to wait until her father had left the house, because he hated the phone worse than this guy did.

"Hello," the voice said again, louder this time.

"Ah, Mr. Divine?" I asked, bolting from where I'd started in the kitchen, as far as the cord would let me, to a corner in the back by the laundry. "Is, is Brenda there?"

"Who's calling?" he asked. I couldn't blame him. I should have introduced myself right away, like my parents had taught me to do whenever I called someone on the phone, but it had been awhile and I'd forgotten, and I was nervous, so Mr. Divine, who didn't want to be on the phone in the first place, was probably thinking I was some sales guy, or someone who happened to know the names of him and his daughter. Super.

"Ah, sorry, sorry," I said, "I'm Danny Rorro, a friend of your daughter's, of Brenda's, from school. I mean, Academy. Hamden Academy."

I felt sweaty and stupid.

I think he kind of chuckled. "Ah, hold on there," he said.

I heard him call out and then footsteps approached. When she got on the phone, it felt like she had saved me from drowning.

"Danny?" she asked.

"Hey," I said, trying to be kind of cool.

"Hi!!!!" she said, too cool to try being cool.

It felt kind of funny talking to her on the phone, just a voice without her face, but we shot the breeze for awhile, told each other about our turkeys and all that (she had a lot more to say than I did), and finally got around to talking about what it was I had really called about, this great plan I had come up with before leaving school.

"So, ah," I said, "are we set for tomorrow?"

"Well," she started, kind of slow and excited before letting the rest just rip out, "I talked to my parents and I practically had to beg, but they said it would be OK, if I called them as soon as I got there and then again before I left. And I have to leave before dark. I mean, because I've never taken the train to the city by myself before, but I told them I'd be meeting you, and that you grew up there your whole life, and that you knew your way around and everything, so, and, oh, I have a cousin who just graduated college, from Smith, and she lives on the Upper East or Upper West Side, I forget, but I spoke to her and have her number and address in case, you know, something happens, so, yeah, yeah, I can come. I can come. I can't wait!"

She sounded so young and adorable and anxious to see me. I felt powerful.

We figured out her train schedule and decided what time to meet at the information booth in the middle of Grand Central Station. After we hung up, I paced around downstairs for a bit, happy as I'd ever been in that big, lonely house. Suddenly, I wished I'd agreed to go with Pop to his stupid football game.

———

I paced around the information desk in the middle of Grand Central Station. It was just a circular booth with a clock on top, but everyone, from everywhere, used it as a rendezvous point. I'd been by plenty of times, and had seen people waiting, nervous, checking the clock or looking through the crowd. I'd seen couples meeting up, jumping all over each other with big kisses and everything. Now it was my turn, and I checked the clock, again and again, searching through that crowd for the first sight of my girl.

People crossed like crazy, but through the blur, right on time, I saw my Brenda Divine. She exited a track platform and made for the clock. I watched as she carefully walked the marble floor in the wide-open room. Her hair was curled against the shoulders of her camel-hair coat, and she was wearing a black skirt with matching tights and knee-high boots. I bet some people were envious of the person she was going to meet.

Seeing me, she smiled so wide I wanted to run over and tackle her.

"Hi!" She squealed, and gave me this huge hug. She smelled like all kinds of flowers.

"You look great, just great," I said, after we parted. "Though I don't know how far we're going to get in those shoes."

"Hey," she said, with her chin up. "These boots were made for walking."

"They were made for something," I cracked.

"Come on," she took my arm. "Let's go!"

We hit 42nd Street and then let the wave of shoppers pull us down the sunny side of 5th Avenue. Sunlight splashed the sidewalks and bounced off the cars that zipped and jerked along. Smoke drifted from manholes. Salvation Army Santas rang their bells. Brenda smiled as we passed the storefront displays.

"You sure you don't want to go into any of these stores?" I asked when we stopped above the fork at 23rd Street.

"I'm sure, thanks," she said, staring at the wedge of a building below 23rd. "I just love being in the city. It's so…life-affirming."

"You want life-affirming?" I asked, called by the smell of a smoky street stand. "Wait till you get a load of these."

We angled down Broadway, below 14th Street, sharing warm chestnuts from a hot bag. Brenda continued to affirm life, sniffing and looking and listening to everything as I rolled along, feeling like a superstar with her on my arm.

"Hey!" she declared around 8th & Broadway. "We're near NYU!"

I pointed west toward Washington Square Park, and we started in that direction, passing academic buildings and high-rise dorms. A spoke of sidewalk led us into the park, where Rasta guys tried to sell anyone with lungs a nickel bag of reefer. The sunken fountain in the center had been turned into a theater for starving artists. Brenda gave a grizzled guy $5 for a half-assed Neil Young number before we walked out the south side of the park. I stopped her on the sidewalk to make a little joke and impress her with my memory at the same time.

"Oh, so now I get it," I said, clever as all hell.

"Get what?" she asked.

"You came in to see the school, 'cause you're thinking about applying here, and I was just here to, you know, show you around and everything. Oh yeah, I get it... I get it now. I'm nothing but a tour guide."

I figured she'd laugh and bury me with kisses and whatnot, to prove how much she wanted to see me, not some school, but instead she got this real sad look on her face.

"Actually, Danny, I did have a reason for coming in today. I wanted to talk to you about something. And I didn't want to do it at school or over the phone."

A cloud blocked the sun as she rubbed her arm and looked down. A crowd of pigeons fluttered away. I'd never felt so vulnerable in my whole life, my beating heart in the hands of a green-eyed girl. She could have killed me on the spot. I swear. I remembered, last year, when this kid in the dorm named Watson got dumped by this girl named Mila or something. Poor Watson locked himself in his room for, like, three days, crying and everything. I pitied the poor kid, thought he was soft as could be, but he didn't seem so weak anymore.

"Alright," I said to Brenda. "Let's talk." I held out my clammy hands, but she only stumbled back a step. Her face lost some color.

"You alright?" I asked. "You want to sit down or something?"

"No, no, I'm fine," she said. "It's just that I skipped breakfast to make the train, and I haven't eaten anything all day, really, besides the chestnuts."

"Um, OK," I said. "So, just let's forget the whole thing, then."

She kind of smiled, and I felt saved.

"How about we get something to eat," she said. "And then we'll talk."

I wanted to be cool, act real calm and everything over lunch, but there was no way that was happening not knowing what would happen afterward. "We're not breaking up or anything, are we, Bren?"

"No," she said with the warmest, sweetest smile I'd ever seen.

"Say that again," I asked.

"No," she said with the certainty I sought. "We are not breaking up or anything."

"Let's get some food, then," I said, leading her away from the park.

The sunlight returned as we walked down Thompson Street. She stopped me on a quiet corner. "You remember when I told you that?"

"Told me what?"

"About wanting to go to NYU. That was the first day we met and you were asking me all those questions. Remember?"

I laughed and held her elbow. "Let me tell you something, Bren — I remember what you were wearing that day."

She blushed and gave me a big, fat kiss, one of those straight-on jobs, all lips. It felt so good, and I didn't want her to pull away, but she did.

"I could tell you how you wore your hair that day, too, if you really want to know." She kissed me again, and I held her there for as long as I could.

—

We crossed Houston Street into SoHo, with its boutiques, galleries, and cafés, and its throngs of people hogging the sidewalks.

We escaped over Lafayette Street into the tip of Little Italy. The streets hummed with both curious tourists and neighborhood people going about their business. In the windows above almost every shop, a Nona kept a watchful eye on the doings below.

On Mulberry Street, restaurant bosses fished for tourists, but we didn't stop until a voice rang out. "Domino!" I looked all around. Across the street was a little guy beneath a big *Ristorante* sign, his hands waving at his sides. "Domino! That you? Get over here!"

The guy with the big mouth beamed as we approached, his hands still out to the side. "How ya' doing there?" he asked as he leaned over to kiss me, with thick red lips, on both of my cheeks.

"Great, great, Ronnie," I said, after the sloppy kiss. "How about you?"

"Can't complain," he said. "I have my health."

"Glad to hear it," I said. "Glad to hear it."

"How's your folks? And the holiday? What about school?" he asked.

"Everything's fine," I said. "Everything's fine."

A Hispanic guy brushed past with a crate of artichokes.

"Is this your place?" I asked.

"Nah, somebody else's," he said with a shrug. "I run the joint for him, though."

"The food's good?"

"Of course!" he said, flailing his arms. "Come on in!"

I started to lead Brenda inside.

"Wait a minute," he caught himself. "Wait a minute. Who's this?"

"This is my girlfriend, Brenda." I said.

"*Scuse* me, Doll," he said putting the reading glasses high up on his forehead. "I didn't even see you there."

"That's OK," she smiled and stuck out her hand. "Nice to meet you."

"Nice to meet you, too," he said taking her hand. Then he grabbed my face and kissed me all over again, on both cheeks. Then he held open the door.

The open space was full of light. The ceiling, high and made of tin, had a fan that turned in the middle. The walls were worn white brick.

"Have a seat right here," Ronnie said, offering us a four-spot in the middle of the room. "I'll be right with ya."

"How do you know him?" Brenda asked. She was all eyes and smile.

I told her about the restaurant Ronnie used to have in the old neighborhood, and how we used to eat there all the time.

"What happened to it?" she asked.

"It closed down."

"No," she said frowning. "Why?"

I loved Brenda. She could care about someone she just met a minute ago.

I shrugged as Ronnie approached with a pen and pad, glasses back down.

"So what can I get ya?"

"Menus would be nice," I said with a wink.

"Ah, Domino," he laughed, trying to bust some capillaries on my cheek with a pinch. "So much like your father." He was tough on the cheeks, that guy.

"I'm just joking, Ronnie," I said, rubbing my face. "What's good here?"

"Everything!" he shouted. "We got some of the best Latin cooks in all of Little Italy."

Brenda and I laughed.

"It's true," he insisted. "I'm the only Italian in the whole joint."

"But the food's good, right?"

"It's fantastic," he declared. "I arrange for all the food – I got beef coming in from Montana, you believe that? Montana! All these other guys around here are serving Jersey cows."

"Good thing" I said. "Because Brenda won't even look at a cow from Jersey."

She kicked me under the table.

"What?" Ronnie asked.

"Nothing," I said. "I'm just kidding around."

"I thought maybe we had one them veterinarians on our hands."

I opened my mouth, but Brenda kicked it closed with another shot to the shin.

"No, no, we're good on anything, Ronnie," I said politely. "What do you like?"

"Tell you what, just sit tight and I'll take care of ya, how's that?"

Brenda and I consulted without words and smiled back at Ronnie.

"Good, good!" he said. "I'll get you started with some vino."

We drank Chianti and shared a platter of olives, bread sticks, and prosciutto. The red wine was good, kind of fruity, and we sipped it as we ate our way through a plate of clams casino that was thick with garlic and lemon and crumbs. We wiped our plates with warm bread. After washing down a bowl of Bolognese with more wine, Brenda was unable to hide the smile that kept turning up her wine-stained lips.

"What?" I asked, putting my glass down on the table. "What is it?"

"Excuse me?" she asked, trying to appear innocent.

"Come on, I can see the wheels turning over there."

"I'm just having fun," she said, shifting her eyes toward the window.

She watched the locals and tourists walk by, but her smile kept coming back.

"Still just having fun?" I asked.

"Sure am," she said, then added, after a pause, "Domino."

"Oh," I moaned. "Thought you might have missed that."

"No chance."

I sipped some wine.

"So?" she asked, with her eyebrows up. "What's it all about, Domino?"

"Oh, *marrone*," I mumbled. "I don't know."

"Come on, Danny," she said, putting her hand on mine. "You never talk about your home or family, and I feel like I'm getting a chance to know you better, that's all."

"I don't know much about your family either, Bren."

We never talked much about our separate lives. We knew simple things, of course, but I didn't dig because, to me, her past was full of boyfriends I didn't want to know about. I didn't want her to know about my history either, so we were still sort of strangers in a way. Not for long, though, thanks to Mr. Face Molester and his cries of "Domino!"

"You're right," she said, "you don't know much about my family, but we're here now with a friend of yours, who calls you by a secret name and says you're just like your father." She sat back and smirked.

"You've had too much to drink, right?"

"Stop trying to change the subject."

"You're reminding me of Meeks right now, you know that?"

She didn't even dignify that with a response.

"OK, Bren." I pretended to be had. "My father's name is Dominick, and people think I take after him and, in Italian, 'ino' is added to the end of a word to mean 'little,' like *uccello* is bird and *uccellino* is little bird, so they used to call me little Dom, or Domino. Domino."

"That's so cute," she smiled. "You look alike, that's it?"

"And maybe we're both funny sometimes, too."

"Oh," she said. "I thought maybe there was more to it than that."

"What can I tell you?" I said. "Now how about a little more wine?"

We continued our slow lunch, dripping honey over Gorgonzola cheese until we couldn't eat another bite. I motioned to Ronnie but, instead of bringing the check, he showed up with a hunk of meat from Montana big enough to feed the whole state.

"*Bistecca per tre,*" he said, placing the gigantic platter on the table. "You guys don't mind if I join you, do you?"

"No, no, of course not, Ronnie," I said.

"Good. You want some roasted potatoes with this?" he asked, squeezing lemon wedges all over the carved steak.

"I don't know," I said. "We've already had a lot." I leaned back and patted my stomach.

"You're right," he agreed. "We'll have beans."

Ronnie stormed the kitchen and returned with some white beans in tomato sauce and another bottle of wine. He filled our glasses and plates and helped himself to a heaping portion. Brenda and I picked at our food while Ronnie cut and stabbed and chewed like a madman.

"So," Brenda said to Ronnie after most of the steak, half the beans, and all the wine had been devoured. "Danny and his father look alike?"

"Those two?" he laughed, while I cringed. "Fortunately for this guy, he resembles his *mutha*."

"Really?" Brenda asked, with her eyes on me. "How so?"

"Don't get me wrong, his father's the greatest," Ronnie said, still chomping away on the food, "but he's a short guy, like me, and, you know, normal looking, I guess, but this guy's *mutha*... this guy's *mutha* is tall and skinny, like him, and what a looker, that one."

My face prickled as my insides twisted.

"You know," Ronnie continued, "around the neighborhood, people called her the Italian Audrey Hepburn!"

"Breakfast at Anthony's," I mumbled. It was the joke our family always made about that comparison.

"They don't call her that anymore?" Brenda asked.

"They might," Ronnie said, tossing a napkin over his bloody plate, "if they were still around."

"Where are they?"

"Have him tell you," Ronnie said. "Now who wants coffee or something sweet?"

"Just a coffee for me, Ronnie," I begged.

"How about you, Doll?"

"Something sweet," Brenda said.

"*Thatta* girl," Ronnie said, and was off for the back.

"What's he talking about?" Brenda leaned toward me and whispered. "Is that why he doesn't have a restaurant anymore?"

"It's a long story," I said.

"Why are you being so secretive, Danny?"

"I'm not."

"Yes you are," she insisted. "And it's so annoying. I want to know what he's talking about, about your name and the neighborhood, and don't get clever."

She was demanding and nervous, kind of like when she bugged me about the wrestlers. I didn't want to talk about this subject, either.

"I'm just trying to save you from a boring story."

Ronnie arrived with a tray full of coffees, liquor, and dessert. "*Allora*," he said, sitting down. "What'd I miss?"

"Nothing," I said, splashing some Sambuca into my demitasse cup.

"Ronnie," Brenda said, sitting up straight, her spoon stuck into a pale-green mountain of pistachio gelato. "Domino doesn't seem to be in a storytelling mood, and I'm curious about what happened to all the people."

"We left."

"Why?"

"Because the Spics came into our neighborhood and took the place over." He said it matter-of-fact, like he wasn't the only Italian in the whole joint. I downed the espresso and asked for the check.

"Sure thing, kid," he said getting up. "I know it's late."

We didn't speak until Ronnie returned.

"No, no, no," I insisted to Brenda as she reached for her black shoulder bag.

"That's right, Doll," Ronnie said. "Yours was free, and his

was heavily discounted." He gave me a folded-up piece of paper. I forked over the measly sum and thanked him for the meal.

"Hey, it was my pleasure," he said, and patted the back of my head. "Tell your folks I was asking for them, and don't be a stranger."

"I won't," I said, helping Brenda with her coat.

"Thanks, Ronnie," Brenda said.

"Anytime, Doll." He gave her a kiss. "Take care of yourself."

We walked outside, but the cool air was little relief to the sickness that filled me. I had lied to Brenda about my name and got caught, which was bad enough, but she also got a taste of what happened back home, what scarred my head and convinced me to change my name in the first place. Wrenched by all these awful emotions and memories, I walked up Mulberry Street, steady as I could, for as long as I could. Then I ducked into an alley and tossed a heavily discounted lunch behind a dumpster.

"Danny!" Brenda screamed as my guts splashed on the asphalt.

I held my hand out to the side, to assure her everything was alright. After spitting the remnants of Montana from my mouth, I bought a club soda from a bodega and took it to a small park on Spring Street.

"Just tell me you're OK," Brenda said once we sat on a bench.

"Yeah, yeah," I said after washing my mouth out.

"Did you drink too much?"

I'd been drinking around the table with my parents since I was 12 years old. I'd never been drunk, or sick, ever.

"It ain't that," I admitted. "But all that about my father and the neighborhood and everything."

"Tell me," she insisted.

"OK," I said. "Give me a minute."

I took some more water. The sun slanted high on the buildings and shadows covered the ground. Under the bare branches of a peeling Sycamore tree, in the cool of a late-autumn day, I told Brenda Divine the story of me and my old neighborhood. When I was finished with the first year of high school, I parted my hair and let her feel my scar with her fingers. She started to cry, right there on the spot. Then she crossed her arms, tucked into herself, and kept on crying, hard, rocking slowly back and forth.

"It's alright, Bren." I tried to console her. "You don't have to cry for me."

"I'm not," she sobbed.

I looked around. "Who you crying for then?"

"All of us."

"What?"

"Nothing, nothing," she said, wiping tears from under each eye. "Please tell me that was the end of it."

I lied and told her it was, figuring the poor kid had heard enough of my sad story.

We sat in the park, with my arm around her shoulder, until dark spots started to appear. We grabbed a cab uptown to Grand Central, for her train to Connecticut and my subway to Queens. After we said our goodbyes and her train rolled away, I remembered she'd come to the city to talk to me. I'd feared that conversation, as soon as she'd brought it up, and figured, now, it couldn't have been that important. I was wrong. Something had had an effect on her, something big, and I couldn't be kept from that.

Chapter 8

On Sunday afternoon, after a subway to Grand Central, I caught a bus going west out of the city. Once the ride smoothed out on the highway, I stared out the window as we rolled along Route 80 and the horizon faded into the cool blue of late afternoon. The trees couldn't go by fast enough. After dark, a reflection appeared in the window, the face of a kid on his way to the place where he belonged. I tapped my feet the rest of the way and practically jogged from the bus stop in town, across campus, and into the dorm.

I walked upstairs, opened the door, and hit the lights. I thought for a second that I had the wrong room. Everything was upside down, or broken, or torn. The mattresses had been stripped and pissed on, our clothes were all over the floor, our desks turned over, and our books and papers scattered like leaves. All my posters were in a crumpled pile in the corner, except for Christy Turlington, who was laid out neatly in the center of the room, a dry stain of pearls down her face and neck. Across the window, in soap, someone had scrawled "THEIF."

I dropped my bags and went for Mr. Wright. He followed me down and frowned at the mess. He didn't say anything for awhile, just rubbed his beard.

"OK," he eventually said. "I will call the custodian and have him bring two new mattresses. In the meantime, Daniel, if you could be so kind as to begin cleaning this up. The van from the airport is due in at around 8. Mr. King can help you then."

"That's it?"

"What more would you have me do?"

"Make those guys come down here and clean this up."

"What guys?" he asked.

I didn't even answer. Just looked at him.

"I think we can chalk this up as a prank, young man. An anonymous prank."

Flipping rooms could be called a tradition at Hamden, and it was kind of normal for a new underclassman to have their room turned upside down. But not a fourth-year student — new or not — and definitely not like this. I thought of Chester's threat that Brenda had overheard: *by any means necessary.*

"Really? A prank?" I asked Mr. Wright without patience or respect. "With body fluids and busted property? Oh, yeah, that's a good one. They got us good, those... those rascals."

"Daniel..." Mr. Wright sighed, but I cut him off.

"Danny, alright?" I said. "I go by Danny."

He must have known I had him, because he didn't even flinch at my tone. "I know this is upsetting, but I have absolutely no means of figuring this out, especially since we were away when the incident occurred."

The wrestling team wasn't away. Winter season sports started the first day back, and the wrestlers spent the holiday here, at school, practicing to the last minute, and probably jerking off in a circle and eating the hearts of small animals. I reminded Mr. Wright of this.

"Well, what would you have me do?" he asked. "Put them

under bright lights for an investigation? Inject them with truth serum?"

"How about a spelling bee?" I suggested, pointing to the window. "That would do it."

Mr. Wright laughed out loud, then looked at the window and shook his head. "I'm sorry, Daniel. Danny. I really am, but I just don't know what to do. I'm afraid if I call more attention to the matter, it will just make things worse. Perhaps if we just treat this as a routine prank, a small fire that we suffocate with silence, there will be no opportunity, no oxygen, for the flames to expand."

He seemed pleased with his metaphor, but I was starting to think that math teachers might be better than these literary-types at dealing with dorms and the things that happen between kids. The eggheads could put all the numbers together, in every possible way, and know, without a doubt, that things didn't add up. I had no faith in Mr. Wright figuring it out.

"Whatever you say," I said to him.

He left me alone with our mess.

—

I worked like a lunatic. After a few hours, the window sparkled and our clothes had been returned to the closet. The desks sat right-side-up, and the books and papers were back where they belonged. I did the best I could, but by the time Terence showed up, it still seemed that something had gone wrong in our room.

"The hell happened?" he asked. He stood in the doorway, his shoulder bag hanging toward the floor.

"Welcome to Hamden Academy," I said, trying to make it sound like a formality.

"What?"

"You're not a real student here until you get your room

flipped — it's a tradition."

Terence walked inside and put his bag down on the bed spring.

"You're not new," he said, looking at the bare walls. Smart kid. No wonder Brown was after him.

"Yeah, well, they must have gotten carried away," I shrugged. My face reddened with shame at my crappy lie.

"Where's the beds?" he asked.

"Ah, we might have to wait until morning for those."

"No, I mean where are the old ones?"

"Oh, they got covered in shaving cream," I said. "I asked them to take them away and get us new ones." I had actually dragged them, reeking of piss, down to the laundry room.

"Shaving cream, huh?" he asked.

"Yep."

Terence looked at the toiletry bag that rested on the ledge next to his bed. It had been untouched. The only untouched thing in the room. Or so it seemed.

"Ah, was your toothbrush in there?" I asked.

"Yeah," he said, picking up the bag.

"You might want to give it a whiff."

He unzipped the bag, took out the toothbrush and held it to his nose. His head jerked back from the smell. He looked sickened.

I walked over with the trash can and he dumped the bag, toothbrush and all, into the bin. "I'm telling you, it happens to everyone. No big deal."

I dumped my whole toiletry bag, too, even though it had been with me all weekend. He stared at me as if I'd lost my mind.

"Someone stuck my toothbrush up they ass, and you're telling me it's no big deal?"

"What can I say? It's a tradition."

"Well that's a messed up tradition right there," he said. "Someone ought to have their ass whooped over that."

He began to unpack. I could tell by the shake of his head that he knew, inside the closet, his clothes were out of order. He looked around the room, wondering what else had been done. He sucked his teeth and made that sound he was so crazy about. No horses came.

I knew that feeling he was fighting, wondering about an enemy that couldn't be seen. An enemy who does to your things what they wish they could do to you. The thought of their hands on your stuff makes you sick, them being in your space when you're not there. Back in Queens, at the big high school, I hated what those pricks did to my locker more than what they did to me. At least I saw their faces when they kicked me around, but I never knew who was scratching messages on my locker or even spitting on me through the crowd. Once, inside my locker, a dead rat was stuffed in my jacket pocket. I had to throw that coat out.

The worst part about this kind of thing is that you don't know who "they" are. And the unknown makes you afraid. It gives you the creeps and makes you think everyone's in on it. You trust no one. You shut down to be safe. Crawl inside. I didn't want to see that happen to Terence. Or to me. Not again.

"Hey, hoops start tomorrow, right?" I said. I lounged across my box spring like it was the most comfortable mattress in the world.

"Yeah," he said, a flash of light in his eyes.

"You want to borrow my lucky shorts?"

"Hell, no!" he said, breaking into a smile.

He let the smile linger. He dug some framed pictures out of his duffel bag and positioned them on his bedside shelf and desk. He tacked a Houston Rockets poster on the wall.

"So, you guys going to be any good or what?" I asked.

"First scrimmage is soon enough," he said. "You can see for yourself."

Chapter 9

The gym rocked during the home opener of the basketball season. It was just a scrimmage, against a nearby prep school from over the Pennsylvania border, but our side of the bleachers was jammed with people yelling and stomping on the retractable stands. Last year, the only noise at our home games was the chirping of sneakers on the hardwood floor. Brenda, Sammie, and I climbed the stands and joined up with a group of kids from our class.

"Hey, where were you guys last year?" I called a few rows down to Meeks.

"No offense, White Shadow," he yelled over the cheer of another basket, "but you guys didn't have T-Money!"

Rice had been blabbing to everyone about Terence's practice performances. I had heard him, over and over, saying that Terence's game was "phat," "stupid," *and* "dope." All good things on his *fagakada* planet. I couldn't help thinking, looking around at all those people cheering and carrying on, that some of this had to do with the fact that Terence was still the mysterious guy who had stood up to the wrestlers. Then I saw a few blue jackets sitting at the end of the bleachers, down from our team's bench. I'd never seen any wrestler at another game. Ever. They weren't cheering or anything, just staring at Terence.

He looked pretty sharp in his white uniform with blue trim. He crouched and hounded some poor kid trying to advance the ball past half-court. When the guy tried to spin away, Terence poked the ball free and was on his way down court.

"Here we go again!" Meeks jumped up and called as Terence swooped to the hoop and finger-rolled the ball over the rim. The room roared. Terence got right back on his mark and swarmed all over him again. The other team's coach called time out.

Our team flopped to the sideline like a pack of puppies. Terence didn't seem all that happy, though, and he covered his head in a towel while resting on the bench.

After the break, the teams went back at it for a few minutes until the halftime buzzer went off. Our guys stormed the locker room, and I noticed, even with all the commotion, that Rice found the time to hang a sweaty towel over Chester's head. He stood and fired it back, but Rice kept running, wagging a finger in the air. The floor was empty, but the gym was still alive.

"He's really good," Brenda said, tightening her fingers around mine.

"Yeah, but he's got, like, eight inches on that kid."

"He should have stayed in Short Hills, then!" Meeks yelled.

"Isn't that where you're from?" someone asked him.

"Damn skippy!" he roared. "I think I know that pud!"

Super. People went on and on about our team. No one noticed when the wrestlers got up and left.

Right after halftime, we had a 30-point lead or something, but Terence still played like the other guys might make a comeback. All that mauling of the opponent's point guard got Terence his fifth foul and a seat on the end of our bench. He's lucky someone didn't file for a restraining order. He sat there on the end of the bench with a towel over his head. I'd seen enough.

Outside, nothing moved in the grip of December. The air, with no scent, stung my nose and ears and neck. The tree limbs were like gray snakes under the low sky. The cloud cover wouldn't break until March, at the earliest. We walked up the path, past the shack and toward Brenda's dorm.

"Well, what did you think about your roommate?" Brenda gushed. "Wasn't he amazing?"

She had her arm clutched around my mine, hugging me so close our breath mixed. I could feel the excitement in her step. It was hard to keep balanced.

"Yeah, he was great," I said. "The whole team looked good."

"Wishing you still played?" Brenda asked, nudging into me.

"Nah," I said. "It's a better view from the stands. Plus, I got to leave early."

"Why did we leave? It was so much fun in there, all those people cheering. It was like being at a college or a big high school somewhere."

"I don't know," I said. "Something didn't seem right. I mean, it was just a scrimmage, but it seemed like more than that. You know?"

"No."

"Never mind," I said, not wanting to get her started with the drama of our dorm. I'd gotten the mattresses downstairs without notice, and hadn't mentioned the flipping to anyone. Terence, of course, could be counted on for silence, though he seemed a little tense, like every time he walked in the room he expected a mess. I knew how he felt.

Brenda and I cut across the meadow, the stiff grass shifting under our feet.

"Are you free at all during the break?" she asked.

"Um, yeah," I said. "I'm wide open."

"Good, because I was thinking maybe you could come up for New Year's."

I stopped in the middle of the meadow and took her elbow in my hand.

"Come up where?"

"To my house, my home, in Connecticut."

"Where are your parents going to be?"

"They'll be around," she said, and walked off without me.

I kept pace a few steps back.

"You'd have to sleep in my little brother's room," she said.

"Alright," I agreed, from behind. "But you might want to warn him about my underwear — there ain't much to it."

"He'll sleep downstairs or at a friend's."

"Probably for the best."

When we reached her dorm, she faced me at the foot of her steps. "So, you want to come?"

"Sure thing, Bella Faccia," I said, wrapping my hands around the small of her back.

"Good," she said, taking my ears in her mittens. "Because I still need to talk to you about something."

"Let's talk right now," I said. "You're my favorite subject. I could talk about you anytime."

"That's sweet," she said. "But I don't want to do it here, at school. I want to be home."

Thinking about where Brenda lived, her house, her town, her room, made me feel very privileged.

"Can I ask you something?" Brenda interrupted my imaginary parade through her world. "Didn't it feel good to talk about what happened to you?"

"Yeah," I cracked. "I feel 13 again."

"Danny!"

"No, it did. It did. I feel kind of, I don't know…"

"Happy?"

"Yeah, happy, I guess," I shrugged. "But not just that."

"How then?" she asked. She leaned into me like I had wisdom to share. Now that was a good one.

"I don't know. I had this feeling like the world had it out for me, you know? Like I was from a different place or something, and different rules applied to me, and at any time, someone could just say 'boo' and I'd crack into a million pieces."

"And you don't feel that way anymore?"

"Not so much," I admitted.

"What?" she asked, squeezing my hands. "Why are you smiling?"

I didn't even know I *was* smiling.

"I don't know — it's stupid," I said quietly as a group of girls giggled past.

"Come on, tell me!"

"You have to promise not to laugh."

"I promise," she said.

"Alright," I said, and looked around. "It's just that I sort of feel, sometimes, like I'm a character in a comic book or something, who once had all this power, and then lost it, but now it's coming back again."

She stared into my face without expression. I waited for some kind of response, afraid I had just sold myself out as a lunatic or a kid still waiting on puberty. She kept that empty expression. I swallowed as she leaned toward me and whispered, "You don't really think you're a superhero, do you?" Then she broke into this huge smile.

"Oh, see!" I threw my hands in the air. "That's what I get for sharing my secrets!"

"I'm just joking," she hugged me, still laughing. "I swear!"

"Alright, alright." I playfully fought her off. "But just for that, I'm gonna show up at your parents' house with my superhero costume on!"

"No, no," she begged, crumpling onto the stoop.

"And let me tell you another thing — there ain't a lot to it, so they might want to, you know, spend the night downstairs or at a friend's house, too."

"Stop!" she cried and stomped her feet.

I hadn't seen her laugh like that all year. She quickly wiped away tears before they froze to her face.

"Alright," I agreed, bumping her as I sat down. "Only if you promise to forget I told you that."

"I promise," she nodded, calming herself.

We sat on the steps, hunched over our knees with puffs of smoke in front of our face. She tucked her arm inside mine. "I'm really going to miss you during the break," she said.

"You, too, but it's only a couple weeks until New Years."

"Promise to be good while you're home?"

"I'll see what I can do," I said.

⸺

The night before break, Terence seemed electric. The hoop team's success, and the support of that success, had him acting a little more relaxed, a little more alive. Still, it had to be tough, being so far from home. His bags had sat piled next to the door since morning. That night, he paced the room and talked as I stuffed my backpack with dirty clothes.

"First thing," he said, rubbing knuckles into palm. "First

thing I'm gonna do is go see my girl, make up for some serious lost time."

He stomped to his desk and handed me the framed picture. "That's Tonya, man. She fine." He didn't have to tell me that. I'd seen her, sneaking peeks when alone in the room. She was beautiful — black skin and white teeth, bright eyes, slender with straight hair curled into shiny, wide ribbons for the prom, her and her red satin dress tucked into Terence, who was wearing a tuxedo. He took the picture back and returned it to his desk.

"And then, yo, it's off to see my boys."

He didn't hand me the picture of them, but I felt like I knew the four of them, including Terence, grouped together, mugging for the camera, making silly gestures with their hands. They seemed like pretty nice guys who had been friends for a long time.

His pictures always made me a little sad, but I looked all the time. I had no pictures of my own.

"And Moms be cooking up a storm, all week, man," Terence continued.

He picked up his ball and dribbled it across the room.

"Is that your family?" I asked, nodding toward the desk, pretending I hadn't seen the picture before. He dropped the ball and brought me his family in a frame — mother, father, son, daughter — all sweaters and blouses and perfect smiles in the perfect light. Other people had pictures in their rooms, but Terence was the only one with the classic shot. They seemed so happy. The American family.

Terence went back to bouncing his ball and imagining his homecoming as I looked at the picture, like it was the first time. Then I asked him something I'd been wondering about all along.

"Your mom's white?"

"What?" he yelled, barging back from beside his desk. "The

hell you talking about?"

"This," I said, pointing at the picture. "She's white."

She had sort of smoke-colored skin with a bob haircut. Her surefire smile said she could do anything.

."You crazy, man," Terence insisted, taking the picture from my hands. "You know that?"

"Maybe, but what's that got to do with your mom being white?"

"She ain't white!" he demanded in my face. "She's light-skinned, that's all."

"Alright," I conceded, halfheartedly. "If you say so."

"Damn right I do!" he said, walking back to his desk. He put the picture back, picked up the ball, and cradled it as he sat.

"Never mind then," I said.

He shot the ball in the air a few times.

"Your sister's cute," I said, back to packing.

"Yeah, thanks," he mumbled.

"She looks like your mom," I noted.

"Mmm-hmm," he nodded.

"Except she's black."

He jumped up. "My mother is black, you simple-ass fool!"

He reminded me of the angry horse-caller-guy I'd met in the lobby on the first day of school.

"Relax," I said with raised hands. "I'm just breaking your shoes a little."

"Yeah, yeah," he cooled himself. "I know."

"You sure?" I asked.

"Yeah," he said leaning back in his desk chair, shooting the ball in the air again with an exaggerated flick of the wrist. "Mom's Creole, that's all."

"What's a Cree-hole?"

"*Cre-Ole*, man," he huffed. "Don't you know nothing?"

"I guess not," I said.

"Creoles is folk from down around New Orleans," he said. "They a mix of Africans and French, mostly, and they ran New Orleans back in the day."

"That's how you know French."

"Yeah, I had some in school, too, but Moms is fluent. She teaches up at Baylor University, so we speak it at home all the time."

"We speak Italian at home sometimes, too, but it's more like 'listen to me or I'll smack you in the mouth,' type stuff," I joked.

"Oh, yeah," he laughed, "we have them talks too, but they all in straight Negro... if you know what I'm saying."

"Probably better than French."

"You got that right," he nodded. "Besides, Pops don't play that French business anyhow."

"Now he's black." I nodded toward the picture.

His father was black as the black of a brand new blacktop.

"Yeah, Pops so dark you can hardly see him on a cloudy day."

"I don't know," I laughed. "He looks sort of hard to miss."

"He's a big man," Terence said proudly. "Played some ball back in the ABA, too, and I can't wait to school his old butt when I get home." He bounced me the ball. "You must be looking forward to getting home, too, to the NYC," he said with a knowing smile.

"Oh, yeah," I lied, like my big city life was full of excitement.

Chapter 10

Being at home, especially for long periods, was still tough for me. The house itself stood as a great big sign of defeat, since it had been bought to keep me safe. Then, after we moved in, each room was filled with argument, silence, and regret. I hid out in my room, the third floor attic space. There was still some funk in the room from the hours, days, months I had spent alone there, and especially from that moment Pop had found me bleeding.

Two years later, the marks on my knuckles and the back of my hand were barely noticeable, and I didn't think of my room as a fortress anymore. I had learned to like my little space. Colored light came through the small, stained-glass window. The walls were slanted and I had set my single bed across the middle of the room with a dresser at the foot. The old floor bowed as I walked around, tending to the posters that had come loose in my absence. I pressed them back in place. The old radiator hissed and, when cranking the knob, I noticed a jewel box that had fallen under the pipes.

I pulled out the disc and dropped it into the player on top of the dresser. A piano tinkled a nice little melody and Springsteen began a story about being a kid and getting older. I figured it was a song about standing up, too, so when the rhythm picked up, I stood up, too, and strummed along with an imaginary guitar and sang all the words to "Growing Up."

I played this song all afternoon in my room, keeping an eye on the clock so as not to be surprised when Pop came home. No surprises for him this time, either.

———

Pop, being a teacher, was on break, too. Things were better now, but we had our moments, and it could still be tough when the two of us were alone. It could be stiff and uncomfortable, like we didn't really know each other anymore. He'd usually come around and ask me some question, like "How's it going, Pal?"; and I'd say something back, like "Good," and then, usually, after some silence, I'd go to another room. That's how it was when we were alone together, and that's why I dreaded the shopping trip I had agreed to take with him to get ingredients for our Christmas Eve dinner.

"You got the list your mother left?" Pop asked on our way to the bus stop.

"Yeah, Pop."

"Read it to me."

"We went over it in the house already."

"Just read it, will ya?"

I read him the grocery list while we waited for the bus. He looked so funny with his olive skin, cleft chin, and bumped nose, his stocky upper body wrapped in a brown bomber jacket. A pork-pie hat tilted back on his head, letting some brown curls fall from his widow's peak. Blowing in his thick hands, he listened to me read the list.

"*Baccala*," he interrupted. "Why every year with the *baccala?* You know what a pain that stuff is, Pal?"

"I know," I said, "but it's tradition."

Italians keep from meat on Christmas Eve, and make up for

it by having every fish in the sea instead, or at least seven of them, including salted cod, or "baccala," as the old-timers called it.

"Tradition?" Pop complained. "You gotta soak that stuff for three days to get the salt out. Then, after all that rigmarole, you know what you got? Cod. Why don't we just have fish sticks? Call Gorton's, we'll start a new tradition."

"OK, Pop. I'll put it on the list."

"Good boy," he said.

The sun was out, but the cold air stung. The sky shivered like blue ice beyond the bare trees and telephone wires.

"You know," I said. "We could have walked to the Flushing market by now."

"Don't start with that again," he warned. "We buy our fish every year from Marrone & Sons. That's a tradition we're not breaking. It's important, and time for you to start coming along again. What's it been, three years since you've been to the neighborhood?"

"Why can't we just drive?" I asked. I could see our car in the small driveway of our large Tudor house.

"What, we're too good for the bus now?" he asked, twitching his shoulders. "Besides, you can't find a place to park over there anymore."

"You could double-park while I run inside."

"And let you have all the fun?"

"Fine," I said. "I'll drive and you can sniff the fish with Mr. Marrone."

"How many times I have to tell you?"

"Tell me what?"

"The reason we go to the old neighborhood, on the bus, to buy fish from the guy who's been selling it to us for 20 years."

"I know, Pop," I said, rolling my eyes. "It's a tradition."

"Hey," he warned with a back of his hand to the top of my arm. "You might want to forget where you came from, but it's important to remember. There's something to that, no matter how you feel about the place now."

The bus lurched down the block, jerked to a stop, then hissed as the doors folded open. Pop gestured, as always, for me to go first.

"I know, Pop," I repeated, before climbing on board.

"You don't know nuts," he said to my back.

After wishing the driver Happy Holidays and dropping our fare in the box, Pop sat next to me and tapped his wedding ring on the back of the empty seat in front of us.

"Look," he said turning to me. "I didn't mean that. There's a lot that you know, but there's also a lot that you don't know. You know?"

"Well said, Pop."

"I'm not kidding, Pal. I worked with teenagers for a lot of years, and I can honestly say that the one thing you all have in common is a certain amount of ignorance."

"What a nice thing to say to your son."

"Hey, I didn't make it up. It's the truth. You want to know the worst part about it?"

"Not really."

"The worst part is that none of you knows it. In fact, it's just the opposite. Don't worry. You'll learn."

"Can't wait." I said, with my eyes out the window.

"You, probably after the others," he said, nudging me.

"Oh, now I get it," I said, turning toward him. "The reason we go to the old neighborhood, on the bus, to get salty white fish from the same guy every year, is so you can have the opportunity to tell me what a dope I am."

"This time," he said, picking up his tapping routine. "Let's not make it part of the tradition, though. Alright, Pal?"

We scored our bounty from the sea and walked the main avenue of our old neighborhood. Pop nodded or smiled at some of the people we passed on the street, stopping to talk with a few. We didn't recognize most of the people, though, which was weird, because we used to know everybody. We walked past familiar buildings that didn't seem to know us anymore. I could still feel it, though, that same concrete under my shoes, the asphalt in my veins.

The people were a little darker than us, and there seemed to be more of them. More cars, too. The metal garbage cans on some corners spilled over with trash. I heard music, and the only time you heard music before was when someone got married, or that time in '86 when the Mets won the World Series. Almost everybody spoke in Spanish. People were out on the street, shopping and mixing it up, just like we used to. I got sad thinking about the way things used to be. I missed my home.

My thoughts vanished, on the spot, when I saw these three girls coming down the sidewalk. They were about my age, and had dark hair and dark eyes and soft-brown skin. They wore down jackets over pleated Catholic school skirts and nylon socks up to their knees that were red from the cold. With locked arms, smiling and laughing, they came closer and closer. The one in the middle stared at me. She was beautiful in a friendly, exotic way. When they passed, she said something I couldn't make out, but it must have been funny because all the three of them girls cracked up. She turned her head between her two friends and smiled back at me. I thought about chasing after my very own "Rosalita," until Pop came back and pulled me along. At the end of the block, Pop went into a place to pick up lunch. I stayed outside the shop, across the street from the string of two-family A-frames, each with a little porch and patch of concrete inside a low iron fence. I looked at our old house.

I remembered running from our door, jumping down the steps and hopping the fence to join the pack of kids waiting for me. I remembered my mother on the porch, talking and laughing with the neighbors and the ladies in the window above the pastry shop across the street. I thought of all the hours in the alley beside our house, playing catch with Pop until it was too dark to see. I smiled, thinking Pop had it right — it is important to remember.

Next to the sandwich shop was an open door. It used to be an insurance office or something, but the sign was gone and someone inside worked on a ceiling panel. Across the room, four old guys sat around a card table slapping down dominoes. Music came from a radio. I couldn't make out much because of the dark, but in the light of the doorway sat a little kid. He had some pieces from the game that he slowly set up. He balanced the first piece on its end. Then, not too far away, he lined up the second. Then, the third piece, he placed just right. He paused for a moment before knocking them all down: bop, bop, bop. He did it again and again, and I kept watching. After a few turns, something struck me. "Yeah," I said. "Yeah."

I realized, right then and there, that those pieces were like people, and if one falls down or stays up or doesn't do anything at all, it affects somebody else, which affects somebody else, and so on, and there you have it. On and on. Good or bad or whatever, it was why Pop always said to do the right thing, because it goes down the line, just like the effect of dominoes falling. I started to think of all the things I had done or hadn't done, and the effect of all those things, good or bad or whatever, when Pop poked his head out of the shop door.

"You coming in or what, Pal?" he asked.

"Yeah," I said. "I'm coming." And just like I used to, I followed my father, right in line: bop, bop.

⎯

People from all five boroughs came to Vito's Latticini for sandwiches, homemade cheeses, sausages, you name it. Cured meats hung from the ceiling and the shelves were lined with fresh pastas and sauces and imports from Italy. Through the glass in back, you could see the guy making the cheese, stirring the steaming tub with a wooden paddle. The salty smell filled me with sweet memories. I had lived across the street all my life, and worked there, on and off, since the 4th grade.

The Mozzarella Sisters, as Pop named them long ago, came from behind the counter to greet us with kisses and hugs and questions, always questions, about how well we'd been eating and behaving. I hadn't seen them in years, and they went crazy over how much I'd grown, how handsome I'd become. With flour-dusted hands, they tugged and stabbed and barked at me, like Italian ladies do: tough like that, but always with a ton of heart. I missed the sisters. I missed my job and the smell of their shop.

After they got done with me, they moaned a little about the changing of the neighborhood but, to tell the truth, they didn't seem all that much worse for the wear. They brought us some just-made mozzarella, which Pop asked them to put on top of the roast pork sandwiches he'd ordered. We took our bags, said our good-byes, and rode home in silence on the bus.

Back at the house, the cod was left to soak, and the six other types of fish were all stored proper, before we spilled our bulging Vito's bag on the kitchen table and got to work. Oh man, the taste of that roasted pork, cut thin and slathered with gravy and mushrooms over the mozzarella — I felt like rubbing it on my chest.

"You got all your college applications in?" Pop asked after a few sloppy bites.

"Yep," I answered from a full mouth.

I'd gone to the guidance counselor after Thanksgiving. We'd talked about my grades and extra curricular activity, my other interests and whatnot, and I'd left there with a handful of college applications.

"Tell me the schools again?" Pop asked.

I went down the list for the umpteenth time since he'd cut the application checks.

"How come I didn't hear St. John's on that list?"

"I'm not going to St. John's, Pop."

"Why not? It's a good school, and it's right here near home. I went there, your mother went there, for two degrees, no less. They owe us."

"Hey, Pop," I said. "I didn't have a bad time today, but that doesn't mean I want to be around here again."

"You wanna go back to school next week?"

"Yeah," I choked.

"Then do yourself a favor and send off an application to St. John's."

"Whatever," I said, dropping my sandwich to the plate.

"I'll tell you another thing," he said, wiping his hands. "I don't care where you get in. I'm not sending you away again unless I think you're ready."

"What?" I asked, my head starting to spin.

"You heard me," he said, taking a bite.

"You can't do that!"

"Who are you talking to with that tone?" he asked, chewing slowly.

I cursed under my breath. Pop swallowed his food.

"*Ascoltame*," he told me to listen in Italian, tugging on my earlobe until I jerked away. "I lost the argument with your mother about sending you to sleep-away at this private school, and the results on that aren't in yet, but come the end of this year, if I don't think you're ready to be away from home again, at college of all places, then you're not going, simple as that."

"What will I do?"

"You can do lots of things," he shrugged. "Go to St. John's or another school around here, get a job. There's lots you can do. This is America."

"Come on, Pop," I begged. "You can't do that."

With his elbows on the table, he laced his thick fingers. "I don't know what they're telling you over at that school, but going away to college is a privilege, OK? In fact, going to college at all is a privilege. I had to do time in the service in order to go, and your mother had to wait until she was a grown woman. So if you think you're going just because your parents can afford it and some school says they'll take you, you're way off the mark."

My drowning dreams and burning intestines forced me to make a face.

"Make that face if you want," Pop said, "but you have to earn the right to go to college, and I don't care what the other kids are doing. That's between them and their parents. What happens with you is between you and me and your mother."

Another face wasn't going to help me any, so I put my head on the table.

"Hey," he said, taking my chin in his powerful grip. "I believe in you, Danny, you're a great kid, and I know you had some tough times, but you gotta get over them or them memories are gonna eat you up. *Capisci*?"

I slowly removed his hand from my face, though I had to admit, it felt good there. I sat back and frowned.

"You're doing alright, Pal," he said, nodding. "Just keep it up."

"How do you know how I'm doing?"

"It's my job to know these things," he said with a wink. "Now help me with this food."

After some silence around the table, I asked Pop if he thought I was a decent enough human being to go away — for one night — to Connecticut. He laughed and said I was. We finished our sandwiches together, like we had a hundred times before, and I couldn't help thinking back to when Pop was my hero.

Chapter 11

I fidgeted for three hours on the train, flipping through magazines. As I got closer, the seaside and the coastal towns relaxed me enough to establish some sort of cool as I stepped into the arctic air. I squinted, trying to adjust to the blinding light.

Brenda waited under cover in the center of the open platform. She had on a tan cowboy hat and a massive down jacket. It felt like I hadn't seen her in years.

"Hey, Sweetie," she sang. "I can't believe you're here!"

"Me neither," I said, giving her a hug. "I've never been to the North Pole before."

Our breath came out in huge clouds, and it seemed like everything around was ready to shatter from the cold.

"Come on," she said, taking my arm.

We climbed into a shiny black Jeep Wagoneer and slammed the doors. Brenda started the car and the dashboard lit up like rocket ship. The Bangles played.

"You got a CD player in the car?"

Brenda nodded.

"You got any other CDs?"

She shook her head. I blew into my hands and rubbed them together in front of the vents.

"Here, I have something for you," Brenda said. She lowered that "Manic Monday" song and motioned to a small package on the dashboard.

"I thought we weren't doing gifts"

"Don't worry," she said. "It's nothing really."

Inside the package — covered with red paper and wrapped in a green ribbon, was a black wool hat. She snatched it away to put on my head.

"Ohhh!" I laughed as I looked in the rearview mirror. "You're a riot, Bren."

"I know you don't like hats, but you could really use one, especially with this cold snap we're having."

"Right now, I'd wear a helmet if you had one."

She put the car in gear and left the station. In her town by the sea, a flock of seagulls swam above the storefronts lit with holiday decorations. A policewoman directed traffic without a whistle. We crossed a drawbridge and drove through winding streets with Indian names. Stone walls curved in front of white-washed homes.

Brenda turned down a lane where I could see the ocean through the trees. The setting sun shot a streak of orange across the horizon. We pulled around a circle at the end of the block and straight into the driveway of the wooden house at the end. Nice place. Two levels with a good-sized lawn out front and a basketball hoop over the garage. A giant wreath hung on a bright red door.

"Hi," Brenda announced to the living room. "We're here."

"Why, hello *thaire*," her mom chimed in a blistering Boston accent. When she darted into the room, my first thought was that Brenda must be adopted or something, because her mother was a mousy little thing with dark hair and eyes. She had on a tomato-stained apron over a silk shirt and black pants.

"*Pleasha'* to meet you, Dan," she said shaking my hand.

"Thank you, Mrs. Divine," I said. "Thanks for having me."

"Of *casse,*" she insisted. "Don't think of it. Now come out of this *foya' befoua'* we all freeze to death."

Brenda hung up our coats in a nearby closet then took me up the short flight of stairs to a hallway that branched off into three bedrooms and a bath. We left my things in her brother's room. Then we went to where Brenda slept. Her double bed had a purple shag comforter piled with stuffed animals. A shelf on the wall held a bunch of trophies. There was a poster of a waterfall with a rainbow over it, and one of a kitten covered in spaghetti. UConn paraphernalia had been spread around. Her desk was lined with framed photos, which I immediately scanned for the presence of boys.

"Whatcha' looking for?" Brenda asked.

"Nothing," I said, straightening up. "Nothing."

"Good," she said, approaching me.

We kissed in the middle of her room. It felt so safe and private and completely overwhelming that I cupped her backside and baby-stepped us toward the bed.

"Oh, no," she insisted, pulling away. "Relax, mister."

"You started it."

"We better go back downstairs," she said. She looked sad, like maybe she regretted bringing me into her home.I followed her down the hall.

In the kitchen her mother stood over a cast iron pot, folding in ingredients from a platter piled with fish. It was a big kitchen with plenty of cupboards and shiny appliances.

"What are you making, Mrs. Divine?" I asked, leaning into the granite counter by her side.

"This is Portuguese fish soup," she said, her head held high.

"We have it every New *Yea's fa'* good luck."

"You're Portuguese?"

"That's right, my *fatha'* was a *fishaman* from Fall *Riva*, Massachusetts."

"No kidding," I said, now understanding the little bit of Mediterranean in Brenda's eyes and skin. I thought maybe I'd been imagining that.

"So, what's in the soup?" I asked, crossing my arms.

"Well, we have mussels, clams, squid, shrimp, some *cawd'*, of *casse*."

"Cod? You mean baccala?"

"That's right!" she said. "You *famila'* with baccala?"

"I'm Italian on both sides. I've had it at least once a year since I could chew."

"Of *casse*," she said. "You have it on Christmas Eve with *yoa'* seven fish, right?"

"It makes my father crazy."

"Not a fish *lova*?"

"Well, it's more all of the rigamarole, like he would say. All the cleaning and soaking and everything."

"Don't I know it," she said, shaking her head.

"Then there's all the courses, which is tough on me, being the dishwasher."

"I'm *shooa*,'" she laughed.

"But it's tradition," I pointed out. "And that's important."

"That's right," she agreed, swiveling her head to look me in the eye. She had this natural warmth that made you want to be hugged or fed by her. Or both.

"Hey, you should give me this recipe," I said. "All we need to do on Christmas Eve from now on is have some soup, and then we can send everybody home."

"I'd be happy to help, Dan."

She called me *Dan*. That cracked me up.

"Thanks," I said, counting with my fingers. "But we need one more fish. Do you put anything else in?"

"Just chorizo sausage, *afta'* the fish is cooked."

"Perfect," I declared. "Sausage is Pop's favorite fish."

While her mother laughed at my unbelievable wit and charm, Brenda eyed us from the other side of the kitchen, sipping a soda. I winked, and we shared a moment interrupted by the slam of a car door. Brenda straightened and waited for her father. He was a big guy with a big head of curly golden hair. His face was a paler, rounder version of Brenda's.

"Hi, Daddy," Brenda sang, rising on her toes to kiss him on the cheek. "This is Danny."

"How are you?" he asked with a flat tone before crushing me with a he-man handshake.

"Fine, thanks," I said, fighting the urge to shake the hurt out of my hand.

He brushed past in a denim shirt and, a mustard-colored work jacket under his arm. He had on construction boots, but they weren't dirty.

He took a beer from the refrigerator, stooped down to kiss his wife at the stove, and walked into the giant family room that covered the whole backside of the house. There was a swoosh-and-pop of a can tab opening, followed by the sound of scrunched leather.

"Don't get too *comfa'table*," Brenda's mother called out. "*Dinna'* will be ready in a minute."

We ate around a table in the corner of the family room. Brenda's brother was away skiing, so I sat in his chair. The soup was good, and I hoped for some of that luck it was supposed to bring.

Her father told me about the building supply & home heating oil company his family had owned for three generations. Mrs. Divine told me how she had met her husband, cleaning and cooking at his fraternity house at UConn. The conversation moved along from school to New York to the fact that they had a party to attend that evening. That got my attention.

⎯

"So, where we going anyway?" I asked Brenda after we'd seen her parents off in their party clothes. The kitchen clock read 11 p.m.

"It's a surprise," she said. "But you might want to bring your new hat."

"Why don't we just stay here," I suggested, looking around the family room with its big, blazing fire, comfy couch, and giant TV.

"I want to be alone, Danny."

"We are alone."

"Yeah, but my parents aren't far, and my father's not much for parties."

"Alright," I agreed. "So where we going?"

"Go get your things and you'll find out."

We bundled up and left through the sliding back doors, down the steps of the deck into the quiet night. The sky was clear and it seemed less cold than during the day. Everything was still. After crossing the stone wall that bordered their backyard, we walked the woods, guided by the moonlight shining through the trees. I wondered what bulged in the knapsack thrown over my shoulder.

"Careful," Brenda warned as we approached a creek that rippled between icy banks. We walked through reeds that snapped against our shins, following the reflected light against the tide until we reached a road lined with little pine trees. Car lights sent our shadows ahead of us as we walked. We stopped in a parking lot. Beyond the cars was a string of small, wood buildings. Above them, in the wide open sky, an enormous moon glowed.

"What's this?" I asked.

"It's our club," Brenda said.

I thought of the time I'd visited Meeks's club. "Where's the golf course and the pool? And the big wooden bar?"

"It's a boat club," she said. "A family club, really. Not very big, but I practically grew up here."

More cars arrived and parked on the grass. Music and light came from the middle building, drawing people like moths.

"I thought you wanted to be alone," I said.

"I do," she replied, and took me by the arm.

We cut between the cars and avoided the music by going around one of the dark buildings. Across the flat surface of the ocean, buoys bobbed and lights blinked at various points in the distance. Just off shore, around the end of a long wooden dock, a dozen sailboats, stripped and covered, waddled in the tide.

Brenda pointed to a rocky jetty that shot out from the shore.

"That's where we go crabbing," she said.

"Crabbing?" I asked. "Sounds contagious."

"It's so much fun," she said. "You tie a piece of hot dog to a string and drop it in the water, and when it moves, you pull it up slowly and then catch the crab with a net."

"Then what happens?"

"You collect them in a bucket and eat em' for dinner." She crinkled her nose. "The fun part's really catching them, since they're sort of hard to eat and there's not a lot of meat."

"Why don't you just cook the hot dogs and forget the whole

thing?"

"Oh, Danny."

"I'm just joking," I said, thinking of my summers on concrete. "Sounds fun."

"You like the beach, right?"

"Yeah, but I didn't bring my suit."

"I know how to keep you warm," she said, leading my by the arm.

We jumped off a small barrier wall into the stiff sand. The water lapped up about ten feet away, delivering moonlight with each wave.

"Isn't it beautiful?" Brenda asked.

"Yeah," I said. "Now where's that warmth you were talking about?"

She took the pack off my shoulder and unfolded a thick blanket. After sitting down, she broke out a thermos and filled two mugs with a steaming liquid that smelled like boiled apples. She passed a cup and covered our legs.

"Happy New Year, Danny," she toasted.

"Happy New Year to you," I raised my mug in return.

I sniffed the strong contents, took a little sip, and reared back. "What is this?"

"Fermented apple cider."

"If by fermented you mean spiked, I'm following."

"It really keeps you warm, doesn't it?"

"I'm not ready to go swimming," I said before having another sip. "But I'm getting there."

"Drink it slowly, Danny," she warned. "It's strong."

"No kidding," I agreed after another sip.

"OK, now," she said, reaching for my mug. "Let's take it easy, because we still have to walk home, and my parents will be waiting up for us."

"I'll be good," I promised, and put the cup of rocket fuel in the sand beside me.

She told me to lean back. We lay on our backs, holding mittens and looking at the jet-black sky dotted with a thousand stars.

"It looks like somebody spilled a bag of marbles on the asphalt," I said.

"Very poetic, Danny," she laughed.

"Yeah, I have a way with words."

"I have some words for you now," she said without moving. "The something I wanted to talk to you about, back in New York."

I had been thinking on the train ride, as I'd gotten farther and farther away from the city, that she wanted to confess her love for me at home. What else could a lovely Connecticut girl have to confess?

"I know what it is," I said, sitting up.

"You do?" she asked, springing up like a car seat.

"Yeah, I do," I said. My heart felt like a little frog trapped in my chest as I sat there looking at her for a few seconds. "You wanted to say that you loved me, right?"

She collapsed back onto her forearms. That went well.

"I didn't mean to wreck your moment or anything," I said. "I just figured I'd make it easy on you. That's all."

She struggled to catch her breath.

"You OK?" I asked.

"I'm fine," she said.

"That was it, right?"

"Yeah, Danny," she said. "That was it."

"Good," I laughed. "You had me scared there for a minute."

She reached for my arm. "I do love you, Danny."

"I love you, too," I said.

Brenda shimmied back against the barrier wall. She covered her face and began to cry.

"You OK?" I asked.

"Yes," she said, but she couldn't stop shaking. I blamed the cold, and the emotions that could stem from a word as big as love. I put my arm around Brenda and held her close, completely clueless about the real reason for her tears.

The air was still, and the sound of waves was washed away by the voices from the party. They came outside and began to count down from 10. I leaned in toward Brenda just as it approached midnight, and our lips met on zero. There were cheers of "Happy New Year!" Some honking sounds came before a fireworks display: pop, pop, pow... boom.

"How's that for poetic?" I asked.

"Not bad," she said, sniffing away more tears. "Now tell me you love me again."

"I'll tell you 10 times if you want."

"Once is fine," she said, snuggling into me.

"I love you," I said as the sky filled with light.

*Ten times...*I said to myself.

Chapter 12

No one was going to write a song about it, but I was in a Connecticut state of mind. I didn't know if it was the sky, the air, or the way the sky looked through the air, but everything up there seemed so bright. So close. I wanted to bounce a ball off that moon. I wanted to live in a town by the sea.

Back at Hamden, I paid the guidance counselor another visit and learned of a school in Connecticut called Stonington. It was up there on the coast, small and private with a pretty good Division II baseball team. I'd never heard of Stonington College, but Hamden had apparently been sending kids there for years. Who knew?

I imagined myself walking across their leafy campus, with all the good-looking students, climbing the big stairs to the columned academic building as the clock tower bonged out the hour. On weekends, I would parade my gorgeous girl from UConn around, showing her off at parties to all my friends and teammates.

To avoid any problems with Pop, I paid the application fee myself. To avoid Pop altogether, I made plans to go for a scholarship. I found out the name of the baseball coach and sent him a letter bragging about my talents. I asked the coach at Hamden to send something as well, and told him not to be shy with the flattery.

I kept this dream to myself, tucked in my pocket with some of that Connecticut moonlight.

Next to my desire to be with Brenda (only every second of every day) came a craving for the kind of friendships I'd had as a kid, and then again with the guys at school last year. I'd never really appreciated the importance of friends until I didn't have any. And now I had some.

Things were cool with Terence. The routine of basketball kept him busy, and campus stayed quiet during the winter months. I made a point of popping in on Meeks and Grohl and hanging out with Sammie once in awhile, too. I was a regular social butterfly, and on an off-day from basketball, I brought the whole gang together for an afternoon at the Can.

Winter at Hamden is a drag — long and cold and gray — and the Can was full of people like us, tired of spending so much time in the dorm. After ordering up and settling into a back corner booth, I prompted this story from Meeks about how he got booted out of the house and into boarding school.

"So I come home one night, you know, just as the sun's coming up," he began. He sat at the end of the table, in a chair turned backwards between Grohl and Sammie at the end of the booth. "And I'm creeping down the hallway toward my bedroom, right?"

"Yeah," Rice followed. I sat on the inside, against the wall, across from Terence who sat beside Rice. Both of them paid attention. Santos, next to me, nodded at Meeks. I kept an eye out for Brenda, because we were supposed to meet, but I couldn't see anything beyond the high backing of the booth.

"And my stepmother comes out of the bathroom," Meeks

continued, "and she's like, 'Are you just getting home, Geoffrey?' And I'm like, 'No Chippy, I fell asleep watching TV downstairs.' And she's like, 'You slept on the couch downstairs?' So, I say 'Yeah,' thinking what a clever devil I am, until she says, 'That's funny, I slept there too, and I didn't see you.'"

"Ooooh, man," Terence laughed with the rest of us. "That's good, but I know they didn't send you away *just* for that."

"No," Meeks confirmed. "But we can get into the rest of it some other time."

Meeks had a whole catalog of outrageous stories about his suburban shenanigans.

"Chippy's a reasonable lady," I couldn't resist saying.

"Yeah," Terence said, a sour look on his face. "*S'up* with that?"

"What?" I asked him. "You never met a 'Chippy' before?"

"I don't even know what that shit is," he said.

"We have a 'Peachy' in my town," Grohl added. "She's hot."

"Hey, yo Chippy or Peachy or whatever your name is," I said in a *Ghoombah* accent. "Get over here, would ya?"

"No, no, it ain't like that," Terence corrected. "It's, 'Yo, Yo, Chippy girl, shake that sweet thing over here.'"

"Get outta here," I said with a wave.

"Come on now," he begged. "Everybody knows black folk is much cooler than the *I-talians*."

"Forget you," I told him. "No chance. The Italians invented cool."

"Oh yeah," he challenged. "How y'all greet someone from 'round the way?"

"How you *doin'*?" I asked in a velvet tone, adding a stylish nod-wink combo.

"*'Sup*?" he delivered in a relaxed drawl.

"That's not even a word!" I said.

"Neither is *'doin'*," Meeks was happy to point out.

"Hey," I warned him with a finger.

"I'm just saying," he laughed.

"Alright then," I said to Terence. "How do you just write something off?"

"*Jccht*," Terence hitched. "Later for that."

"Not bad," I admitted, "if you don't know how to say, *fagettaboutit*!"

"Pa-lease," Terence waved me off. "Later for that."

"*Fagettaboutit*!" I bounced back.

"You got that one," Sammie was happy to tell me.

"Oh man, Sam," Terence protested. "I thought you was *my* boy."

Sammie blushed.

"Let's settle this," Grohl said, setting his elbows on the table. "One more for the title, OK?"

"Cool with me," Terence said.

"Shoot, pretty boy," I said.

"In the most succinct and complete way possible," Grohl posed, rubbing his hands together, "put someone down."

"Yo mama," Terence said to me, circling his head around.

"Ooohhh," the judges cooed, as they took turns slapping Terence five.

I struggled for a response as they counted time, "Tick tock, tick tock."

"Time's running out there, Chief," Meeks informed me.

"Can't I get back to you on this?"

"No!"

"But he got to go first!"

"Come on, Danny Boy!" Rice sang. "Man up, G."

"Alright," I agreed, before thinking out loud. "Your mama… Your mama… Your mama MIA!" I said, shaking my raised hand. "Mama Mia! Get it?"

They bounced French fries off my face. Terence smiled, pleased with himself.

"Fine, fine," I said, "but the Italians are still the coolest."

"Aw, you *trippin'*, son," Terence said.

Rice concurred.

"Oh yeah?" I challenged with my forearms on the table. "How about DeNiro, Pacino, Vinny Barbarino! Ralph Macchio, better known as the Karate Kid." I jumped up from the booth and did the crane pose from the movie. The guys howled. Terence smirked.

"All those greasers just pretending they cool on TV," Terence said, his mouth tucked to one side. "Besides, Denzel Washington could act all those fools under the table any day of the week."

"OK," I said. "Whatever."

"Look, man," Terence said smugly. "For cool, there's a simple rule: if ya wants to be down, you gots to be brown!"

The guys all laughed hysterically, shoulder bumping and slapping fives, despite the fact that it excluded them, except for Santos, sort of, from coolness.

"Oh, OK," I said. "I see. I see. So by that logic, my mother is cooler than yours."

The table went quiet. Terence's eyes pulsed a few times.

"Yeah, you see, my mother's straight Sicilian, and I can tell you right now, she's more than a few shades darker than that lady in the picture on your desk."

Terence reared back as if violated.

"Oooohhhh," the fellas cooed.

Terence jabbed a finger at me and opened his mouth. But no

words came out.

"Its alright, T," Grohl said. "Rice's mother is white, too."

"It's true," Rice confessed.

"So's his daddy," Meeks whispered loudly.

"You know what?" Terence barked while we laughed. "Y'all just ignorant, that's all. She ain't white! She's light-skinned, and she's cooler than all y'all's mothers put together."

"Oh, relax," I told him. "We're just messing around."

"Alright, alright," he nodded, up and down, up and down. "But this shit comes up again, it ain't gonna be so funny."

That was true. It would come up again, and it wouldn't be funny. Not at all.

⸻

Brenda saved me from the crowded booth. We followed Terence outside and he went home as the two of us went down the steps of the academic building. Brenda giggled and pulled me along with an urgency that had me curious. Damn curious.

That morning, she had left a note in my mailbox asking me to meet her after school. Valentine's Day approached and her note was covered in hearts. "I Love You" notes had been in my box, randomly, since we'd been back from Christmas break, so I didn't think anything all that crazy was in play until she came for me in the Can with smiling eyes and a secret on her lips.

"What is it?" I asked as we entered a classroom, the same classroom where we had fought earlier in the year. "Tell me," I insisted.

She wrapped her arms around my neck and kissed me tenderly, but we kept getting interrupted by her lips breaking into a smile. Brenda bristled with energy, like a kid on Christmas morning.

I fought off her kiss, held her hands down, and tucked my lips inside my mouth.

"OK, OK," she said. "I did it."

"Did what?"

"I got us a room."

"A room where?"

"At the Yankee Inn in Hackettstown."

My first thought was *why the hell would we want to go to Hackettstown?* My second thought, helped along by Brenda's devilish grin, made my eyes go wide. I wondered if she could hear my heart beat.

Chapter 13

Brenda and I separated our sweaty palms and smiled at each other. The gym rocked on this Saturday afternoon, Valentine's Day. A win by Hamden's hoop team would bring us our first ever league championship and a spot in the state tournament. The game was close, but we had other things on our minds.

I watched the clock more than I did the tight game on the floor. We went along with the clapping and stomping of the bleacher boards, but Brenda and I were out of step with the rest of the crowd.

I wasn't distracted enough to miss Terence, though. He was clearly the best guy out there, like all year long, but now he played even better because the edgy attitude had been dropped. I had gone to every home game, along with half the school, and Terence had starred every time, but he just didn't seem to be enjoying it, scowling and fouling and everything. In the room afterward, he would barely talk about the game.

As the second half went on, Terence, nearly single-handedly, delivered the team to a monster lead, shooting the lights out, taking the ball to the hole or, when double- or even triple-teamed, passing to teammates for easy baskets. He even played a gentler version of his assault and battery defense.

The rout was sealed about halfway through the fourth quarter when Terence stepped in front of a lazy pass and streaked toward the other end. The crowd rose, expecting one of the fancy finger rolls we'd seen all season. Heads went up a little higher when Terence veered from his normal route to the basket. Instead, he swooped to the right and came at the rim from the side, where he jumped off his left foot with the ball cuffed under the opposite wrist. He seemed to float as he drifted higher and higher, knees climbing and the ball sweeping across his twisted torso. After windmilling an arm over his head, he slammed the ball through the rim with his legs flared out in opposite directions. What a sight. It was hard to breathe, just watching. Terence hung onto the rim and pulled himself up before letting go. He landed smoothly on both feet, facing the cushioned backstop. He spun around on his heels and headed back up court with a fist in the air.

Almost everyone, even the guys on the other team's bench, hopped to their feet. The burst of excitement yanked some of the front row crowd onto the floor. The referees blew their whistles and brought all the craziness to a halt. Order was restored and Terence was rewarded with a rest on the bench, which he took without his usual towel-over-the-head routine. He looked pretty proud there, checking out the crowd with a cool smile on his face.

Our fans counted down the last seconds of the game and then stormed the court. The team lifted Terence into the air, and he waved a happy finger, bobbing in the sea of students that buoyed him. I would have liked to join in, but Brenda and I had a date in Hackettstown.

We climbed down from the stands and followed on the edge of the festivities toward the exit. In the area before the doors, two men stood, athletic guys in sweatshirts that said "Brown

University" over the image of a basketball. Now I knew why Terence had picked up the whole "there's no I in team" routine. Smart guy, that Terence.

———

Brenda and I left the gym and crossed campus toward our Valentine's date. We passed the bridge above the crashing water and took the steps into town. On Main Street, Brenda pulled out car keys and unlocked a little blue car.

"Whose car is this again?" I asked, snapping my seat belt.

Brenda rolled her eyes and started the engine. "Tracy Johnson. I can't believe you don't know her. She's in your math class."

"Freckles?" I asked.

Brenda shook her head and shifted the car into gear. We climbed the winding road out of town and joined the empty highway. At the first exit, we took the access road into town. Tire wheels crunched the gravel of the parking lot, popping nerves like corn kernels inside me as we approached the Yankee Inn Motor Lodge, long and wooden and white. I waited in the car as Brenda checked in with her credit card, which she carried on her for emergencies. In my book, this qualified as an emergency.

She came back out, held up the key, and motioned with her head for me to follow. It felt like secret agent business, sneaking around like we were. The room was in the wing just off the parking lot, and I stomped my boots on the walkway as she worked the lock. Quickly, once inside, we closed the shades, flung off our jackets, and flopped onto the queen-sized bed.

"I can't believe we're doing this!" Brenda shrieked at the ceiling.

"I know," I said, sitting up to inspect the room. "You think there's anything on the TV?"

"Stop!" She smacked my leg before rolling off the bed to rifle through the shoulder bag she'd placed on the dresser. Alongside the TV was a tray with plastic cups wrapped in cellophane and a bucket for ice. I wished we'd brought some champagne or something to ease our nerves, because it felt like I was being tickled from the inside by thick fingers.

"What do you think?" she asked after turning around, a silky black thing held over her red sweater.

I (sort of) faked hyperventilation, breathing in and out like a lunatic.

"So you like it?" she asked.

I nodded furiously.

"I'm going to change then," she announced, and then bit her lower lip.

I was now sure, by her nerves, that she'd never done this before either. I'd never asked her, because I wanted to know, but I also didn't. And I definitely didn't want her to know that *I'd* never done it, though I was certain, in that moment at the motel, that all that was about to change. I hopped up from the bed and marched back and forth. I shadow boxed in the mirror, punching the air with hooks, jabs, and uppercuts.

What to do? What to do? What to do? Aha!

I kicked off my boots, ripped off my sweater and T-shirt in one swoop, and fell to the carpet as I yanked off my jeans. When the bathroom door cracked, I jumped up and bounced on the bed in nothing but socks and black bikini briefs. What an outfit.

Brenda looked amazing. The camisole reflected the light that slipped through the drapes. The hem lingered at the top of her thighs. Her hair brushed the spaghetti straps and her bare arms looked skinny and beautiful, especially the soft underside exposed as she touched the door frame beside her shoulder. Her smile was shy, but sure.

She lay down beside me. I kissed her dry mouth with my dry mouth. I slipped a hand under the silk and squeezed her soft hip. She smelled of lotion and candy. Brenda was still, except for her breaths, which were low and rapid. I was overwhelmed, pressing myself into her as I ran my hand up and down her legs. I felt pressure and redemption and wonder all at once. I reached for her again, but she grabbed my arm.

"Don't worry, Bren," I croaked. "I've never done this before, either. I swear."

"It's not that," she said, her voice more hollow than breathless.

"What's the matter then?" I asked.

She pulled back the sheets and hid her body under the covers. "I'm sorry, Danny," she said, her eyes on the ceiling, the blankets clutched to her neck. "I thought I could do this. I want to do this. But I can't without talking to you first."

"I know what it is," I said ready to restate my dueling-virgins theory.

"No you don't, Danny," she turned toward me to say. "You don't know."

Her voice was stern, like an adult's.

"OK then," I said. "What?"

She sat up and kept the covers pulled tight. She freed a hand to hold my wrist. "I don't want you to get upset."

"Why would I get upset?"

"Because it's about Todd."

I sank. I sank remembering them together. He had given her piggyback rides. She'd sat on his lap. They'd kissed all the time. They'd had private places. It had gone on for months. I bet he'd been to her house, and had met her mom and dad. He'd probably sneaked out of her brother's room in the middle of the night like I didn't have the guts to do. I tasted dirty pennies and got upset.

"Are you kidding me with this guy?" I asked. "What's he got to do with us? What's he got to do with anything? And you bring him up now?"

I shimmied off the bed and put on my pants. Brenda wrapped her arms around her legs and rocked. Tears fell from her face like small stones. "Don't go," she said through a sheet of tears.

My heart kind of stopped, but I was no longer the guy who thought about other people before thinking about himself. "I get it. You chose the popular guy over me and, what, he broke your heart or something? He dumped you for somebody better? It happens, Bren. I know. Get over it already."

I didn't really know what I was saying. I was just saying. I struggled into my T-shirt and sweater and boots and then abandoned Brenda for the cold afternoon. Dark clouds covered the sky and the wind burned my eyes. Without my jacket, I headed for the highway.

It took me two hours to get home. I had to walk on the highway's shoulder. Cars honked as they whipped by in the wind. Truckers flashed their lights. On the one-lane road to Hamdenville, I had to step into the weeds whenever a car passed. I figured a little blue one would appear, with a sympathetic honk and begs through the open window to please get in. But I was wrong. No one came to pick me up.

Back at school, Terence was on the phone talking to his parents. He sported a Brown Basketball sweatshirt and a great big smile. No one else was around, so I walked to the shack and sat alone in the cold. It smelled of dead wood. On the way back to the dorm, snow began to fall.

Overnight, a foot of powder landed. I sat in the window on Sunday morning, staring at the snow-covered campus. Split in the middle by the shoveled path, it looked like a book without words.

After brunch, some students showed up with trays from the dining hall and used them to sled down the slope of the bowl. Snowballs were chucked, and a battle began between Montgomery and Carlyle. A lot of guys were out there, even the big basketball star, Terence. Snowballs flew back and forth. Our side could have used me and my pitching arm, but I didn't belong with them.

My mind raced. Thoughts kept coming and coming. I couldn't relax or think straight. A soup of emotions swirled in my head: anger, regret, sorrow, self-pity, concern. I went over the events again and again and couldn't decide whether to cry or to break things. Despite everything, I missed Brenda more than I knew was possible, and I had this sense of being so far away, even though I could see the crown of her dorm. My reflection in the glass resembled a ghost. My teeth chattered and my body ached, so I ducked under the covers and didn't come out until the next morning.

I walked to breakfast in nothing but my thickest sweater on top of my second thickest sweater. My last meal had been Saturday's lunch, only half of a ham sandwich as I'd looked forward to the loss of my virginity in an afternoon delight. That went well.

I wolfed down three breakfasts in the dining hall, then stopped by the mail room before the start of first class. I exchanged the yellow card in my box for a brown grocery bag stuffed to the gills. I carried the paper sack outside and opened it under the Arch.

Inside were both of my jackets and a few other things Brenda had borrowed. I put on my leather and opened the envelope on top of the clothes, figuring it would be Brenda's first attempt at making things right. Another good call by me.

Dear Danny,

How could you leave me like that? Haven't we been together long enough for you just to hear me out? Are you that shallow? Insecure? That much of a JERK? It wasn't about me getting over Todd. It was about me getting over what he did to me.

Last summer he invited me to his house, but when I got there no one was home but him. He said his mother really wanted to meet me and that she had to go away for the night, last minute, and would be back in the morning. I didn't even know his parents were divorced. I should have left. It felt creepy, but he told me how much it would mean to him for me to meet his mom, so I stayed. We drank a little, then started fooling around and he kept saying gross things and grabbing me everywhere, but I kept telling him "no." I just didn't feel like we were ready, and I didn't feel comfortable at all. And I don't remember anything else. Something happened, but I don't know what.

In the morning I couldn't figure anything out. I was dressed and everything, lying in his mother's bed, but my clothes felt different. I felt different. Todd said I passed out on him and he had carried me upstairs, but I wasn't that tired and had only drank a little. He was acting weird and secretive and had this creepy look on his face, so I just went home and pretended like everything was normal. But it wasn't.

I knew something happened, but I didn't know what. That was the worst part, not knowing. What had he done to me? I knew it wasn't my fault, but I didn't know what to do because it was, like, date rape, I guess, kind of. MAYBE? And that's so hard to prove, especially when you don't remember anything, and especially when the other person is everybody's Mr. Wonderful and I was totally there, alone in his house,

*drinking and fooling around and everything. I felt so stupid and so
alone.*

*I called him a few times and he didn't call me back, so I sent
him a letter saying if he came back to school, I would tell everyone that
he did something to me that he shouldn't have. I would tell everyone
that he put a drug in my drink or did something and that he was a
criminal. I guess he believed me.*

*I was a complete wreck before coming back to school, and more
so once I got here, even after I found out for sure that Todd wasn't
coming back. Then I realized I just needed to be near home and
planned to leave and would have left had it not been for us. I needed to
be with you, Danny. I was scared and lonely and thought you were the
kind of person who could make me feel better.*

*For awhile, I did feel better, a lot better. I fell in love with you
and started to feel better about everything. I started to think about
going away to college again, but that would have been a mistake since I
still feel so afraid sometimes, like now.*

*Todd took something from me, and I want it back. I thought
that you could help me, especially after hearing about what happened to
you at home with your head and everything. I was wrong.*

*I hope you realize how wrong you were. How could you leave
me there in that room when I needed you so much? You could have put
your arms around me and helped me feel better, told me everything was
going to be OK, but you didn't. You wouldn't even listen to me. You
ran. You jerk!*

*Do not try to talk to me. We are not together anymore, or even
friends.*

*I realized this is something I have to work out by myself or with
people capable of caring. I suggest you do the same since you clearly have
things of your own to work out.*

I feel sorry for you, Danny. I feel sorry for all of us.

Brenda

Her words landed like a cinder block to the stomach. I dropped the bag onto the slushy ground, doubled over, and dumped my lumberjack breakfast into the snow.

"Ewwww!" a group of girls cried as they hurried past. I grabbed the shopping bag, hopped the snowbank alongside the meadow, and booked it through the knee-deep powder, my heart beating down to my soggy shoes. I'd never felt such panic before.

As I ran, the wet bottom of the bag began to give, and my things started dropping out, one by one, as I destroyed the beauty of the previously-untouched meadow.

I leaped up the stairs of the women's dorm, slid across the deck, then burst through the heavy door with a shredded brown bag dangling from my hand. "Get Brenda, please," I begged through heavy breath. The few people in the foyer looked at me like I was crazy. They were right. "Brenda!" I called to the 2nd floor landing. "Brenda!"

A few minutes later, Brenda's roommate came hustling down the stairs to tell me she wasn't available. I stayed put. Five minutes later, the lady who ran her dorm came down and asked me politely to leave. Then she asked me, not so politely, to leave or she would call security. I didn't even know we had security.

I dropped the last strand of my tattered bag on their marble floor and walked outside. Sweat poured out of me into the cold air. Steam rose. My jeans dragged from the waist down and my whole body felt numb as I retraced the trail through the meadow, picking up what I'd dropped. I walked the path back to Montgomery, my arms heavy with all the things that I carried. My classmates were on their way to first period. I went to bed.

I stayed in the room for two days, sleeping off my idiot's flu. Terence brought me sandwiches and juice from the dining hall, and

Sammie hooked me up with Early Birds. Mr. Wright visited twice a day to check up on me and confirm my excused absence from class. Puking in public usually gets you a few days, and the fever and chills that shook me didn't hurt either.

The real sickness came from the feeling I had about Brenda. I had let her down, abandoned her at the moment she needed me most. I was the opposite of her hero. And because of that, I knew. I knew for sure. She was already over me.

Chapter 14

I'd been up and out of bed for a week or so, but was still overwhelmed by sickness. I walked around like a mope, not really speaking to anyone or doing anything beyond what was required. I could feel myself slipping into the hermit mode I'd been in back home, during my second year of high school. I felt like calling Dr. DeFuso or somebody to tell them how bad I felt about everything. It was jealousy, I guess, and stupidity, I'm sure, that made me treat Brenda that way. But it was more than that, too. I'd disappeared. I wasn't myself anymore. I hadn't been for awhile. And what made it worse was that I couldn't imagine what it was like to be anybody else either.

—

The dining hall at Hamden Academy was a long room with shiny chandeliers. The thick blue carpet matched the wallpaper hung with portraits of former headmasters and etched names of valedictorians. The large windows were framed in dark wood. The L-shaped hall was spaced with thick wooden tables, six chairs per side and one at each end. The seating rotation for the students changed every couple of weeks, while faculty stayed put at the heads.

Every student was required to be at lunch and dinner each weekday, semi-formal at night. Attendance was taken right before announcements, with Sunrises dished out to those who were absent or even late. Behavior was monitored and specific rules, both formal and informal, were law.

"You kill it, you fill it," a perky freshman reminded me after I polished off a pitcher of milk.

I hadn't spoken a word to the others at my table since we'd started up together the previous week. They all went quiet, and their eyes were on me as the noise from the rest of the hall blathered on around us.

"Right," I acknowledged, and stood to fulfill my duty while the others went on with their meal.

I refilled the plastic pitcher in the room next to the kitchen. On the way back, with my head low, I began to think about the stupidity of my zombie routine. Common sense came creeping into my mind, until the pitcher was jerked straight down and a flood of cold liquid splashed over my crotch and thighs. I was soaked with milk. Chester snickered as he walked away. The cold shock that shivered me was quickly exchanged for hot rage.

I snatched up the empty pitcher and drew back my arm. I narrowed in on the target, just as I had been coached in baseball. I was going to bounce that thing off the back of his head, but before I could fire the pitch, I was stopped by a grip to my wrist.

"Yo," Terence said. "The hell you doing, man?"

He had a look of real concern on his face. The whole room was quiet. Heads popped up all over. Everybody stared. I dropped the pitcher and walked out of there, right through the looks and the laughter.

My nerves felt like the lit fuse of a firecracker, and as soon as I got outside, the early March evening started in on my soggy patch. It felt cold down there, for sure, but as I walked, the dark, empty campus began to soothe me. I followed the path slowly, breathing and releasing air in long, steady breaths that drifted toward the darkened sky. Silence seemed to ring.

I sat on the bench in front of the dorm and let the anger and frustration and everything else poisonous inside me swell and rise and then streak down my face. I cried, at first, without sound or motion. Then I bawled like a child, shuddering from spasms. The teardrops fell from my chin, like the blood that had dripped one time from my head, and another time from my hand.

When the tears stopped, I stayed in the stillness, the total stillness, gazing out over the silhouette of tree tops swaying in front the slanted roof from under which the whole school breathed. A wisp of wind brushed across my cheek. Then, just like that, the cloud cover broke. Streaky pieces played hide-and-seek with the slivered moon, and the campus was covered in new light. It was suddenly less cold, too.

Glowing clouds pulled away from the moon. On the pointed tip, I reached up my hand to pierce my finger. Imaginary blood dripped into my mouth. I didn't taste dirty pennies this time, like when I was a kid in the street with my head busted open. This time, I tasted Italian ice, like when I was a kid — a real kid — and those streets belonged to me. I stayed on the bench for awhile, staring at the wide open sky, a finger in my mouth and my eyes on the moon.

———

"Ah, we find you dressed, once again," Mr. Wright teased when he and Terence came into the room after dinner.

"Yeah," I laughed from behind my desk. "We got that going for us."

I'd been sitting at my desk with the chair toward the window, tossing a baseball into my soft mitt. Mr. Wright had come down the path with Terence, so I'd known this time that they were coming for me… not that I'd planned on dancing around in my underwear, anyway.

"I have good news for you, Daniel," Mr. Wright said.

I moved to the window ledge and rested my feet on the trunk between the two desks. Terence came to his desk and sat by my side; Mr. Wright, in the middle of the room, sunk his hands into his pockets. He seemed to be on my side, too.

"Good news for me?" I asked. "This I gotta hear."

"Well," he started, swelling his chest, "I talked them into only giving you two weeks of Sunrises for walking out of dinner."

"Thanks, Mr. Wright." Really, I figured it'd be worse.

"Headmaster Hurley saw the whole thing, as did I, and he was apparently not pleased with Mr. Chester, but the wrestling instructor…" he began snapping his fingers. "What's his name?"

"Coach Cauliflower Ears," I suggested.

"Yes, him," Mr. Wright smirked. "He was able to convince the headmaster it was all an unfortunate accident."

"You don't say?" I asked.

"Yes, not surprising," he added.

"How many Sunrises did Chester get?"

Mr. Wright frowned. "Like I explained. Coach… what did you call him?"

"Cauliflower Ears."

Terence cracked up. Mr. Wright smiled.

"Yes, Coach Cauliflower Ears explained to the headmaster that it was all…"

"Oh, never mind," I waved him off. "I know what you're going to say."

"I imagine you do."

"Those guys have it made. We all know that."

"You can consider yourself quite lucky, also," he said, crossing his arms.

"How's that?"

"Well, if I wasn't there to take up your defense, and your roommate hadn't stepped in to stop whatever you had planned with that milk pitcher, you would have found yourself in a considerable amount of trouble."

"You call that lucky?"

"Why yes — don't you?"

I looked at Terence, then back at Mr. Wright.

"I guess so."

Mr. Wright took a deep breath and kept his chest high as he spoke. "The magnificent writer Flannery O'Connor once said that anyone who survives childhood has enough stories to tell for the rest of their lives."

That kind of sounded true, but maybe not for me. "Yeah," I said, "but I'm no storyteller."

"We all have stories to tell, Daniel," Mr. Wright answered. "And you are certainly in the midst of a very compelling one."

"You don't know the half of it," I said with a huff, thinking about my last couple of years.

"I imagine," he said. "And it's your story to tell, if you so choose."

Maybe it is, I thought. *Maybe it is.*

⌒

Getting up and out the door by 5:30 in the morning was practically torture, especially the first day. But soon enough, I started to get into the routine: the walk to detention in the new light, the hour of daydreaming behind a desk, breakfast afterward by myself, and finally the stop in the mail room before first class.

I liked the feeling of having a jump on everybody else, having been up and thinking two hours before most of them. I needed the head start.

I paid attention to my classmates and started to recognize their patterns, like who was showered and ready versus those messy-haired and frantic. I noticed wardrobe consistencies and fashion disasters.

Watching people became a habit, and I kept it up throughout the day, putting faces together, recognizing couples and groups of friends. I could tell a freshman from a sophomore by the amount of Hamden gear they wore. I learned and remembered as many names as possible.

I missed Brenda like crazy and felt relieved when she began to walk, once again, with that bounce of hers. I hadn't gone up to her or even tried to make eye contact. I figured respecting her request to stay out of her face was like an apology that kept on giving. It was hard, real hard, but my slow awakening had me interested in other things, too — and not just things that had to do with me.

I'd kept an eye on the wrestlers. Not just the jar-heads from upstairs, but anybody I saw walking around in blue jackets. It was the height of the season, and the Wanted posters that had covered the mail room earlier in the year had been replaced with ones about their matches, with the date and time posted up top. On the bottom, it read: Support Wrestling. The notices felt like orders.

I didn't know who'd want to support those guys, because they really didn't talk to anybody. I had originally thought it was just tweedle dumb and tweedle dumber who had the major personality defects, but it was really all of them. They were like a separate, hostile student body that occupied the school instead of being a part of it. When a blue jacket passed, people stopped talking. I could tell the wrestlers dug it, in a small-penis kind of way. In public, they nodded and smirked at each other, and I can imagine the laughs they had in private. It was almost like being held hostage by them, and I wanted to know more, so I paid a visit to a friend in the know.

"Hey, Sammie," I said, entering his room one afternoon. "How's things?"

"Hi, Danny," he said from his desk.

His room was well-organized and neatly decorated. He had personal photos taped all over his closet door. Sammie always looked like a different kid in the pictures he had from home. It was funny to see him smile. The walls were covered with tapestries and posters of sad bands like The Smiths and The Cure, sorry-looking fellas with bad hair and pasty faces that made the grunge guys seem cheery. There were also some freaky art prints by that nut Dali, and a poster of Einstein with a quote underneath saying that real geniuses were misunderstood and hated by the morons. Something like that. Sammie came to the throw rug he had between the two beds.

"What are you doing here?" he asked.

"What?" I responded, acting hurt. "Can't a guy come down to see his pal?"

"Well, it's just that you never do."

"I'm here now, ain't I?" I said. "And I thought you could take me over to see some wrestling."

"What?"

"Yeah, well, there's a game or a match or whatever they call it, and I figured I couldn't be here for two years without at least going once."

"OK," he shrugged. "I guess we can go."

"Good. Grab your coat."

An annex to the gym had been converted into this special little theater for the wrestlers. A steep balcony circled up over the matted floor and the crowd sat over the action. On the mats, both teams warmed up, grabbing and tackling and whatnot. It was kind of dark in there, too, with the only real light coming from the center of the domed ceiling way overhead. "Welcome to the Jungle" by Guns-n-Roses blared on the stereo system. It seemed more like a show than a sport.

The air was sticky and damp as a basement. You could smell the sweat soaked into the rubber mat. Banners from all of the team's national championships hung from the balcony. Sammie led me up there, and we found seats in the back. All the rows below us were filled, but the crowd didn't seem all that excited.

Last year, when Sammie was the manager, he'd come back to the room after the matches and tell me how the place was so packed, and so crazy, that the balcony would shake. Then I'd tell him how the only people who showed up at the basketball game were the JV squad, because they had to, and some day student's older sister, who only came to give him a ride home.

Down on the mats, both teams stalked around benches on separate sides of the room, pushing and talking and pumping each other up.

"Anything I need to know?" I asked.

"Not really," he said. "They go by weight, so it starts with the lights and works up to the heavies."

There was actually a kid on each team smaller than Chester, but he wrestled second against a guy right about his size, another kid you could probably cram into a Chinese food carton. They darted around pretty good, and it was like watching the fighting fish someone had in their dorm room last year, little pokes and bites until one fish slowed down. Chester was the tougher fish that day, and he was way up on points when the other guy just gave out and got himself pinned. Chester acted all tough, breathing through his nose like a tiny gladiator, though it was hard to take him seriously in the outfit. I mean, who picked out the wardrobe for this sport? Between the shoes and those leotards, those guys were about as hip as a bowling squad. No wonder some of the fakes on TV wore masks.

Anyway, we watched some more matches, mostly wins by us, until it was time for the heavies. The last match with Trent McCoy was much more interesting than the other ones, and it made me feel lucky, real lucky, to have walked away from our standoff only minus some dignity, a shirt, and a pair of khaki pants. McCoy was smaller than his blubbery opponent, but he used some scary strength and serious technique to toss this tub around like a sack of laundry. It seemed like he could have ended the whole thing anytime he wanted, but he pulled these moves, over and over, that slammed the poor mountain to the mat, again and again. I think the score was like 44 – 2 when it ended.

McCoy hardly breathed heavy when we passed him on the way out. He squinted at me for a few seconds and shot some air out of his nose, before putting his stone eyes on Sammie. We picked up our step and didn't slow down until reaching daylight.

"What happened with them guys?" I asked as we walked down the path. It was cool and cloudy outside. No signs of life on the trees.

"What do you mean?"

"I thought you were tight with them?"

"No, not really, not anymore," he said like it was no big deal.

There was still some snow in places but, otherwise, the campus was clean and brown. A couple of guys tossed a football around the field.

"Why not?" I asked him.

"Why not, what?"

"Why aren't you tight with those guys anymore?"

"I don't know. I'm just not."

With eyes straight ahead, Sammie picked up the pace toward home.

"Come on, man," I begged. "Last year, when you were the manager, you used to tell me they were alright."

"That was before."

We were up on Montgomery, and I held the door open for him.

"Before what?" I asked.

"Before I heard them saying things about me," he said, breezing through the lobby.

I stood there thinking for a second or two. When I made it inside, Sammie was headed for the stairwell. "Sammie," I called. "Wait up."

He kept on, so I hustled and caught him on the second floor landing.

"When?" I asked. "When'd they say those things?"

"OK," he sighed, turning to face me. "On the first day of school, I heard they were living in the dorm, upstairs, so I went up to see them, and I heard them talking about me."

"Like how?"

"Saying how that loser Soifer lived downstairs, and how I gave them a rash." He said it all very la-di-da. "You know, the same things lots of people say about me."

"Don't say that, Sammie," I said as he walked off.

"See you for dinner, Danny." He went into his room and closed the door. Standing in the hallway, I started to figure some things out. I started to see how the dominoes had already fallen, in a bad way, and how they might fall some more.

Chapter 15

"You hear about Todd?" Meeks asked.

I spun around. He'd snuck up behind me in the laundry room as I dumped some threads in the machine.

"What about him?" I asked.

He dug his hands into his pockets and looked shifty. "Follow me," he said.

I left my dirty clothes and trailed Meeks into his corner room. Grohl waited empty-handed, his guitar leaned up against the wall.

"What about him?" I asked again.

Meeks sat in his beanbag chair and locked his fingers behind his head. "He's gone."

"Gone where?"

"He doesn't live at home anymore."

"You breaking my shoes?"

"No, no. I went there, to his house, and his mother told me," he insisted.

Suddenly, I was the one greedy for gossip.

"When? When? What'd she say?"

Meeks dished about how he'd been calling Todd every couple

of weeks since school started, leaving messages on his private line, until the line was disconnected. Home for the last weekend, Meeks took a cruise up to Todd's town in Westchester, NY. He went to Todd's house and knocked on the door. His mother showed Meeks in and told him that Todd didn't live in their big old house anymore. She told him that a pretty girl had shown up and told her that her son had done something horrible and that his mother should know. That was it.

"Who was it?" I asked.

"She wouldn't say," Meeks answered, perturbed. "I even asked her to, you know, describe her or something, but she wouldn't say anything beyond the fact that the girl was pretty. Big help that is. Every Betty that Todd dated was pretty."

I knew who it was. I could tell by the way Brenda had found her step. She'd taken back, best she could, what had been taken away.

"And the more I thought about it," Meeks went on, "the more I realized it could have been a lot of people."

"How's that?"

"You know, man," Grohl said, "Todd was our friend and everything, but he always had to have whatever he wanted, especially with the Bettys. He's the one who schooled us in the rules of cat chasing, and he took more than a few girls from both of us, especially this sorry-looking dude."

"Bite me," Meeks said.

"So?" I said. "I thought all was fair when it came to that crap and you guys?"

"It is and it isn't," Grohl said. "Todd took it too far sometimes, and he kind of had this reputation."

"For what?"

"For the rope-a-dope," Meeks said, kind of mischievous and

kind of sad, too.

"The hell is that?" I had to ask.

"Man," Meeks sighed. "You city boys are rubes, you know that?"

He was right about that, in a way. These suburban kids were into things I knew nothing about. So Meeks explained this drug Rohypnol and how sick guys think it's cool to drop it in girls' drinks and have their way with them when they're passed out. Super. It made me feel lucky to have grown up middle-class, under the eye of my mother and father and everybody else in the neighborhood. It also made me sick thinking about the girls this had happened to, especially Brenda Divine.

I asked about Todd and how he'd gotten this reputation, so Meeks clued me in.

"When we were sophomores, there was this senior girl, a super hot fox named Bernadine Thompson, and Todd had been after her, like, all year, but she wasn't having it. At the end of the year, there was a big graduation party at someone's house for the seniors, and Todd was there, of course, and she says he gave her the rope-a-dope."

"How'd she know?"

"She woke up in one of the bedrooms with a hangover."

"So?"

"She's doesn't drink. She's allergic to alcohol. And she wasn't planning on spending the night."

"OK…" I nodded.

"And Todd was next to her on the bed..."

"And?"

"When she got home she realized her underwear was on inside out."

I felt sick.

"Bernadine told her parents," Meeks continued. "And they called Headmaster Hurley."

"And what'd he do?"

"You know who Todd's father is?

"All Todd ever said was that he was an asshole who lived somewhere overseas or something."

"He is an asshole. A rich one. He runs an investment banking firm out of Switzerland."

Grohl said that Todd's father had come to Pride Day the previous year, arriving by a helicopter that landed on the soccer field just before the game started.

"He came all the way from Switzerland for Pride Day?" I asked.

"Well," Meeks coughed. "He sort of had a private meeting with Headmaster Hurley, too. Apparently, some funds were exchanged in order to keep Todd in school."

"And how do you guys know all this?"

Meeks scoffed. "We find things out. It's what we do."

"The freaking Hardy Boys," I said.

They smiled and slapped each other five.

"So what made this time different?" I asked.

"Whoever it was went straight to Todd's mom, and Mrs. B already knew about Bernadine Thompson, too, of course. And the way she was talking when I was there, it seemed like there could have been some other times, too."

"There's a reason," Grohl said, "that a connected cat like Todd Brooks goes to Hamden Academy and not one of them Harvard high schools in New England."

"Super," I moaned, feeling bad about the world. "So where is he now?" I asked.

Meeks grinned. "Military school."

"Say that again?"

"You heard me," he said, still grinning. "Military school! I guess Mrs. Brooks put her foot down or his father had enough of bailing Todd's ass out. I don't know. But that boy is the property of West Point until he turns 18!"

I wanted to kiss Mrs. Brooks. I also couldn't help thinking that if I hadn't played my cards right back at home, Todd and I could've met at military school instead of at boarding school. At least at military school, I wouldn't have had to worry about him stealing my girl. Or hurting her.

Poor Brenda. She didn't deserve what happened to her, of course, but she had stood up to him and maybe stopped some other people from getting hurt. That took a ton of guts. She had taken care of things on her own, the best she could after the fact, but there was still a little something I could do to keep her secret safe.

"I know it wasn't Brenda," I lied.

The Hardy Boys questioned me with their eyes. "You sure?" Meeks finally asked. "We were thinking something was up with her, you know, and him not coming back to school this year."

"Must have been somebody else," I said. "She dumped him over the summer, fair and square. No big deal."

"How do you know?"

"She told me," I said. "She must have figured that guy out first, smart as she is."

"And what about you?" Grohl asked. "She figure you out, too?"

"Yeah," I said. But I was going to work on that.

I went upstairs and wrote a letter. I wrote a letter to Brenda that didn't mention anything about Todd or anything about me. I only asked for her to let me know she was OK with a smile or something.

I sensed a new beginning toward the end of winter. A warm wind danced around campus. Some flat clouds still hung overhead, but there was enough sunlight to make the new air sweet and easy to breath. My dreams were of those incredible things that usually fill a teenager's sleep. Sometimes, I'd be sad after waking up, but during the day, I walked on green grass and thought about tomorrow. I thought about those things I had been denied, those things I had denied myself but still had coming.

I had other things to do besides dwell on myself and my future. I had work. Piles of schoolwork they dumped on us every day, assignments in history and math and other big-book stuff. I read. I wrote. And I monkeyed around with decimal points even though 'rithmetic gave me a rash. And somehow, through the hassle of college preparation, I found time to think of Brenda. Her face and her smile filled every dull moment, every lapse in concentration.

Connecticut, that little state I had never thought about before, became my symbol. My dream. And it was there that I would make good. I'd get a scholarship to Stonington College and impress my parents with my maturity. I'd make new friends and be good to them while working on getting back my old friend, with her beautiful face.

Signs of spring began to arrive, squirrels and birds and buds on trees. And even though it was still a little cold, and it still got dark early, I felt the looming spring had good things coming. So I waited for winter to quietly close.

The basketball season ended on the road, in the first round

of the state tournament, and they lost by a lot. According to Rice, Terence had his worst game of the year. "*Homie* barely showed up," were his exact words. I swear. Future sportscaster, that kid.

Terence didn't care. Compared to how private he'd been with most everybody all year, he went around now like the Pope on parade, smiling in his Brown sweatshirt, talking to people here and there. I guess you couldn't blame him. He'd gotten what he wanted out of Hamden: a full scholarship to an Ivy League school. Not bad.

But before he could put away his high-tops, there was one last game. Every team that makes the state tournament gets to play against the faculty. It's a tradition, and not such a bad one, since it's kind of fun to get out there in front of the whole school and make the teachers look foolish. Last year, we played them in softball and ran those old-timers into the ground. Wrestling gets skipped, of course, though it would certainly be something to see… especially a rematch between Mr. Wright and McCoy. I'd be the first one there for that, hoping that Mr. Wright had a weapon hidden under his sweater.

Anyway, the teachers played the basketball team on a Friday afternoon. The school made a pretty big deal about it, since it was the first time in a long time we'd done anything in basketball. Wrestling season was still going, and they were on their way toward the state championship before going for the national title. Still, people seemed more excited about basketball.

Both sets of stands were filled, and I hoped to catch Brenda there, with that smile I'd asked for in my letter. But she didn't show. There were a lot of blue jackets, though, spread out through the crowd in groups of two. I wondered about the spacing, since those guys ran like wolves. I wondered why they were there at all.

The scene on the floor was something else. The two

basketball coaches were fairly young guys who still had some game and style, but the rest of the teachers were a wreck — old sneakers, bandaged knees, padded elbows, even some goggles and headbands. I was even embarrassed by the lack of material in some of the shorts they wore. And they played worse than they looked. It was like an old-timer's reunion of the worst team ever.

The real team dressed in their own gear, with most of them following Terence's style of baggy shorts and cut-off sleeves. Since the coaches were on the opposing team, Terence ran the player's side. He directed all his guys around, made substitutions, and even got booed when he took himself out for a minute. Everyone loved him, and he ate it up, smiling and encouraging people, even trying a couple of half-court shots (one of which he made).

Mercifully, the game only lasts two quarters and, by the end of the first, it was like the Harlem Globetrotters vs. those stooges they beat by 100 points every time. When they started up again, Terence came out on the teacher's side, and a little bit of a game began. Terence got the old guys involved, and the crowd cheered as they sort of made a comeback. Some of the teachers even started talking some smack to the youngsters, best they could, at least.

It was a lot of fun. Everyone cheered and laughed and it felt, for the first time, like we were a real school with real pride and camaraderie and all that. I got kind of sad for a second, thinking that this was the last year. Then I got back into watching the game.

With the lead down to 10 points, Terence switched back to the player's side and the rout was on. He caught an alley-oop pass and slammed it home, hanging on the rim with his feet dangling above the poor art teacher's head. Next time, he did a fancy spin move in the lane and dropped in a floater. Later, when the teachers surrounded him, Terence threw blind passes to wide open teammates, mostly Rice decked out in shorts suited for a flag pole.

With only a few minutes left, the teachers gave up and handed the ball at mid-court to Terence. He smiled and started toward the basket in that same way he had in their last home game, when he'd topped his dynamite performance with a crazy, twisting dunk. Just like before, he swung out to the right and approached the basket from the side. I, like everyone else who was at that last game, knew what he was up to and sat up to watch. But there would be no crazy, twisting dunk this time. No finish at all.

When Terence was a few feet from the basket, in the dead quiet of a gym tight with anticipation, one of the wrestlers jumped up from his seat and yelled, "Your Mama's white!"

The ball bounced off Terence's foot and rolled away as he skidded to a stop. "Your Mama's white!" Another wrestler stood and yelled from the other side of the gym. Snapping in the direction of the other voice, Terence stood there all alone on the empty side of the court. I felt helpless and out of breath.

"Your Mama's white!" A third *turd* in blue stood up to yell from the far corner. It was Chester. McCoy stood right next to him. They stared at Terence.

It was as silent as our dorm on the first day of school when the wrestlers were waiting on Terence to say something. That same frozen scene seized the gymnasium, with all eyes set on Terence. Not just the dorm, but the whole school this time. He looked around as some teachers gained their senses and climbed the stands for the wrestlers, but Terence didn't stick around. He stepped toward the nearby exit and started running before he reached the door. I jumped from the bleachers and went after him.

———

I hauled ass down the path and barged through the Montgomery doors. After racing up the steps, I walked into the room, huffing hard. Terence breathed heavy, too, as he paced back and forth beside the window. When he turned and saw me, his eyes flared up. I put my hands out to the side. He charged and grabbed the front of my jacket.

"What are you doing?" I asked, being slammed into the closet door. "Get *off a* me!"

I grabbed his wrists and tried to free myself, but he wouldn't let go. His eyes were round and red at the edges. I could smell the sweat and hot breath coming off him, and my hands slipped off his forearms.

"It was you that done that," he kept saying. "You."

I didn't know what the hell he was talking about, but I knew this wasn't the time for questions. I drew my hands from his waist and broke his grip around my neck. I pushed him hard in the chest. He punched me in the mouth, and I tasted blood as my shoulder crashed into the closet door, knocking it off the hinges. I whipped off my jacket as he shifted for another punch and was barely able to duck in time. I tackled him to the ground. We landed between the beds and wrestled like maniacs on the tiled floor. As we rolled, back and forth, my elbows and knees smashed into the hard surface. It hurt like hell, but I kept going.

I did my best to get the upper hand, but Terence had so much rage it felt like I was fighting three guys. His arms and legs were everywhere, getting leverage off every surface, using his size and strength to spin me over. Punches landed on the back of my head. The sound of knuckles filled my skull. I flashed to getting beat by those guys back home and dug down for some anger of my own. An elbow over my shoulder caught Terence in the jaw and knocked him off of me. I lunged for his face with my thumbs aimed at his eyes when Mr. Wright came flying into the room.

"Stop it, stop it, stop it!" he screamed.

For some reason, I listened. I didn't want to do this. I didn't want it at all.

I pushed off of Terence's face and made sure his head caught some ground. He jumped to his feet, but Mr. Wright stood between us. "I will call the police and have you both arrested if you don't stop this right now!" Mr. Wright kept us separated with his arms out to the side. He breathed almost as heavy as we did.

"What in the world is going on in here?" he asked.

"I didn't do anything, Mr. Wright," I said, panting and pissed off. "I came in here to check on this guy and he starts throwing punches." Spit flew from my mouth as I spoke, and I could still taste blood.

Mr. Wright turned to Terence. "This has been a very, very challenging afternoon for you, Terence. I realize that. What happened back there was totally unacceptable, and I will personally see to it that those responsible-"

"He's responsible," Terence yelled, pointing over Mr. Wright's shoulder at me.

"Me?" I screamed. "The hell did I do?"

"You told them that crap about my mother!"

"I didn't tell nobody nothing," I said.

"Where'd they hear it from then, huh? Where'd they hear it from?"

"I don't know," I said. "Maybe they heard us clowning around that day in the Can. They could have been sitting right behind us for all I know."

Terence calmed for a second, then flared up again.

"Yeah, but you're the one who started with that shit in the first place. Then you and the rest of y'all racist chumps ran with it."

"Racist?" I asked. "You're the one who cares about that crap."

"Oh yeah, right, right," he said, with his chin raised. "Why don't you just call me a nigger and get it over with."

"Ah!" Mr. Wright screamed in reaction to the forbidden word. Panic plastered his face.

"Hey," I said to Terence. "That must be your word. It ain't mine."

"Hell it isn't," he said. "You just don't got the guts to say it 'cause you're scared of what it'll *getcha*." He pointed at my lip.

"Ah," I waved him away. "I know nuns that hit harder than you." It was true.

He started to step around Mr. Wright. I crushed a fist, ready to start whaling.

"Oh, no, no, no, no!" Mr. Wright yelled. "I let you both speak. Now this is over. One more punch or push or shove out of either of you and you will be immediately expelled. I promise you I will see to that. I promise you that."

Terence gave me a bring-it-on look. Mr. Wright steadied himself. I thought about getting on with it, but then I thought better. I was smarter than that now.

"Hey," I said. "I'm not going back to Catholic school for nothing, especially not a dumb-ass like you."

I walked out of the room and waited outside the door for Sammie, already deciding that we'd be roommates again. I was back where I'd begun at Hamden Academy.

Chapter 16

No one spoke much at all about what had happened. And no one asked about me being down at Sammie's, since it seemed obvious that Terence needed solitary confinement. He was like a kid on fire, walking around with flames coming off his clothes. I couldn't believe he stayed at school.

Mr. Wright called me in for a meeting. We sat at his desk in the front hallway. He told me how he was going to keep this fight a secret. You gotta love these private schools: all rules and almost as many exceptions. I didn't complain, since it was nice to be part of the exception for a change. Though I was surprised Terence saw it that way.

Mr. Wright explained that there had been a long phone conversation with Terence and Mr. and Mrs. King. And while my former friend and roommate was ready to hit the road, like I'd figured, his mother had other plans. He would stay at Hamden Academy until graduation, and then his butt was going to Brown. End of conversation. Sounded like the chats I'd had with my folks.

Speaking of which, Mr. Wright had a conversation with my father, too. So much for the secrecy. I didn't have to be there for their talk but, afterward, I was told to call home. He handed me the phone and walked to the back of his apartment.

"Hey, Pop."

"How's things, Pal?"

"Not so hot."

"I heard."

"So, I guess I'm in trouble, huh?"

"I don't know, are you? Mr. Wright told me what happened, and that he was chalking it up to, ah, what did he call it? Extraordinary circumstances."

"That I know," I said. "I meant with you — I guess I'm in trouble with you."

"I don't know, Pal. Sounds like a tough situation."

"Extraordinary?" I asked, with a heavy dose of optimism.

He laughed. "Yeah, maybe, Pal. But I'm not as interested in labeling it as I am in making it right."

"How am I going to do that?"

"First of all, I'm assuming this guy Terence is a friend of yours, right?"

"Yeah, I guess he's my friend," I said. "Or he was."

"Good. Then you should be able to figure out where he's coming from."

"Houston?"

"OK, that's a start. And where's he going?"

"Get this, Pop. The guys got a free ride to Brown, an Ivy League school, and somehow he's bent out of shape about it."

"You have any idea as to why?"

"I'm not exactly sure, but I think it might have something to do with the fact that he's mental or something." Pop didn't laugh, and I was sorry I'd said it like that. I wanted Pop to help me figure this whole deal out just like used to, so he mostly talked and I mostly listened.

"Mr. Wright tells me this Terence is an African-American, the only one in the school, and that he had a lot going for him, and the world is calling him. And his parents must know it, and somewhere inside he must know it, too, or he wouldn't have done what it takes to get into a school like Brown."

"So?"

"So, for some reason, he's struggling with it."

"Struggling with what?"

"You know, I've worked with minority kids for 15 years, and one thing that some of them share is a real resistance to the world outside their own. And if you think about history, and even the way things still are, it's not so hard to understand why. So maybe this Terence is struggling with all that, with who he is and where he fits in."

"I don't know, Pop," I said.

"I think you do, Pal," he answered right back. "I think that you do."

He was right. I knew what it was like to be an outsider, or, at least to feel like one. I thought about Terence. It'd been a long time since I'd thought about what it would be like to be anybody other than me. No wonder I had such a hard time figuring things out.

"So, you see where he's coming from?" Pop asked.

"I'm working on it," I said.

"Good. It shouldn't be such a stretch for you, Pal. And remember, you were brought up to look out for other people. If you're in a position to help someone, you're supposed to do it."

"OK, Pop," I said. "I got it."

I hung up the phone and thought of the dominoes again, and how I could help Terence from falling the wrong way.

———

Sammie sat crisscross on the floor, switching up CDs. I sat

in the window, pounding a ball into my glove and looking out over campus. A week had passed since the conversation upstairs with Pop. April had arrived, but spring and everything after seemed secondary to making things right with Terence.

Around the dorm, he was Godzilla, breathing fire and looking for trouble. Outside, he bumped kids in the hall, skipped meals, and piled up Sunrises left and right. Someone had to save him from himself, which wasn't going to be easy, since you couldn't get close to the kid. I avoided him, since I knew that, if we went at it again, I'd be done for sure at Hamden Academy. And while I wanted to help him and everything, I still had plans for next year. Big plans.

A bunch of wrestlers, all the ones who'd stood up during the basketball game and yelled, including Chester (but not McCoy), had been suspended for a week, though their punishment wouldn't begin until after their season ended. Unbelievable.

"Please, Sammie," I begged, as he began to plug in another gloom-rock album. "Any more of those crybabies and I'm moving down to the laundry room."

"Let me guess," he said. "You want 'Thunder Road,' right?"

"There you go," I said with a wink. I'd been playing a lot of Brenda's favorite Springsteen song lately. And after a quick trip in my head to the Connecticut seaside, I went back to smacking the ball into my glove and thinking about Terence.

I understood where he was coming from, I really did. I'd been hurt, too, and it messed with everything. All your hope goes away, and you think of the world as unfair and vicious. It practically makes you blind. And it definitely makes you stupid (especially in my case).

And I knew Terence blamed me like I blamed my father, because we have to blame someone for our suffering, and the easiest person to blame is usually right in front of us, though rarely responsible. And I knew that it wasn't just me and Terence who suffered. It was part of growing up, and almost every kid everywhere goes through it in some way or another, including those we never think of, even though they're sometimes right in front of us.

"Hey," I said to Sammie. "Let me ask you something."

"Sure, Danny," he said. I could tell he was kind of happy again, having me back in his room, and I hated to scare the crap out of him like this.

"You still have them shoes, or did you get rid of them already?"

"What shoes?" he asked, trying to look all perplexed, though he knew, right away, what I was talking about.

"The wrestling shoes."

He jumped up. "I don't have them!" He said it in a voice about two notes higher than normal.

I hopped off the window ledge and walked toward the middle of the room to turn off the music. "Bullshit," I said. "At first I thought it was that retard Rice, but that was before I figured out it was you who stole them shoes."

He stood up and faced me, for the first time, with confidence, like he knew he was smarter than me. He was, but I had him here.

"You know how I know?" I asked.

"How?" he said, daring me

I walked over to the closet and put my finger on the door. "Right here," I said. "This picture right here. That's how I know."

He came over and squinted at the photo of his friends from home, caught in some hilarious moment with Sammie right in the middle, sunglasses on and his head thrown back in laughter, *wherethehellishamdenville?* printed across the front of his shirt. My shirt.

"I'm sorry, Danny," he said. "It must have gotten mixed up with my laundry before we left for the summer, and I forgot to bring it back. That's all. So what?"

"That was my lucky shirt, Sammie," I said. "You knew that."

His eyes were wide, and the little giblet under his chin wobbled.

"Why'd you take my shirt, Sammie?" I asked. I was right in his face now.

"I didn't," he said. "I didn't."

I asked him again. When he opened his mouth, I cocked my fist. He collapsed on his bed.

"I'm sorry. I'm sorry," Sammie yelped. "I was so mad at you. I was so mad. I thought we were friends and you dumped me. You dumped me for those jerks. Didn't you know how mean they were to me? Didn't you know how bad that made me feel?"

He buried his face in his hands and began to cry. I didn't need to think for a second about what he'd said. I knew. And I told him so, and that I was sorry. Then I sat right next to him on the bed and draped an arm over his shoulder. We sat like that for awhile.

Chapter 17

Spring showed up for real, with showers and flowers and all that, but a dull sense of something, like an invisible fog, hung between our young heads and the new blue sky. It kind of felt that way ever since that whole deal with Terence and the wrestlers, and while Terence practically disappeared, the wrestlers were everywhere. They'd won the state tournament, and were into the regional semi-finals. If they won the northeast part, they'd be going to the national finals somewhere in Missouri or something.

I knew all this because of the announcements they made practically every night at dinner, and the new banner that hung from the Arch and, of course, because of the *fagakada* signs they kept putting up in the mail room: Support Wrestling. I started to think the same genius who designed their uniforms came up with that slogan, too. I started to think that the students who didn't wrestle, and who didn't like being told what to do and when to do it, needed a slogan of their own.

The point would be that we were tired of being second class students, tired of being bullied, tired of having our school divided by a minority of knuckleheads who didn't even care about the rest of us. Pop had taught me to stand up and do the right thing, and standing up to the wrestlers seemed like the right thing to do. It reminded me of back home, in the old neighborhood, when things started to go wrong. If more people had stood up, the outcome would have been different. Much different. For everyone, not just me. So I started working on a plan.

One afternoon, I walked off campus, down past the waterfall and into town. At the old general store, I bought a can of spray paint, some duct tape, a box of rubber gloves, a bottle of prune juice, a ball of twine, and a pack of gum. The old lady behind the counter looked at me like I was nuts. She was right. Back in the room, I sat in the window, chomped on the gum and worked out the details. I had to admit, what I came up with was crazier, and more dangerous, than anything I'd ever considered.

Baseball began in the middle of the month. We'd been practicing for a couple of weeks, and the team rolled through some scrimmages against some local high schools. We figured we might be pretty good again, maybe even better than last year. The first league game would let us know for sure.

On the April afternoon that we waited on York, the sky was bright blue with white clouds exploding in the distance. I was the first one on the field.

An untouched baseball diamond is so beautiful. The just-cut grass, fresh-raked dirt, and that white chalk, like cake frosting, always reminded me of my first time at Shea Stadium. I was 5 years old, and the second we cleared the tunnels and saw the field, I knew the world was full of magic. The Mets got smoked that day, 8-to-nothing, but still, Pop and I stayed to the end. We snuck down to the box seats after the big shots left early and sat there, right behind the dugout, eating peanuts until the very last out. I remember that day, and that feeling of wonder, every time I come across a fresh field.

Across the grass of the Far Fields at Hamden, my teammates approached in their blue and white uniforms. Coach warmed us up with some basic drills. We looked good, which was important, since York was supposed to be the best prep team in the state this year. They had smoked us pretty good last year (I think it was 8-to-nothing), and probably expected to do the same that day. I felt a little intimidated when their players appeared around the bend by the gymnasium, taking the 200- yard walk in their red pinstripes.

Our team came to the bench and sat there as the boys from York unpacked their gear and ran crisp drills in their sharp uniforms. We watched from the bench with our hats yanked down.

I called out to my catcher and went to warm up. Behind the bleachers, we tossed the ball back and forth until he squatted to take some real throws. The warm, moist air helped my arm get loose in a hurry. My fastball popped as it hit where I aimed. I thought back to when Pop and I used to play catch in the alley, and he would insist, every time, that I throw exactly where he held his glove. "Focus on your spot, Pal," he would say. "Then hit it."

That day, during warm-ups, I hit my spots alright, like never before. I was worried about leaving all that good stuff on the sidelines, so I gave it a rest and went to each guy individually, shook his hand, and told him we would win. I swore we would.

Our team took to the field, and the guys behind me did their warm-ups while I threw some from the mound. "Play ball!" the umpire yelled, and our catcher fired the ball down to second base, where it went around the horn and back to me. I looked over the field to make sure everyone was in position and then turned to face York's lead-off man.

He got himself ready with tugs on his crotch, squints, and spits. Classy sport, that baseball. I went into a slow wind-up and then snapped off a nasty curve. The batter jumped back just as the break began, leaving him out of place as the ball arched over the plate. "Strike one!" the umpire called. Things got quiet. I missed a couple of fastballs outside, then smoked two down the middle for the first strikeout of the day.

From there, the pattern was set: fastballs and curves, like a one-two punch, working in tandem, each more devastating due to the threat of the other. After mowing down the other two batters, I walked straight to our bench without looking around. I remembered the way the air smelled — clean, with the coming of moisture — but there would be no rain that day. That day belonged to me.

Each inning during warm-ups, I reminded myself of what Pop had told me about focusing first, and then hitting the target. I tried to think about what the batter was expecting. Fastball or curve? Inside or outside? Then, I did the opposite. I felt invincible, like a superhero or something. A superhero and a mind reader all wrapped up into one. Everything moved in slow motion, expect for the pitches, which zipped from my hand to right where I aimed. There was no sound in my world, no peripheral vision. Just straight ahead. After each inning, I walked right to our bench and sat on the end.

We'd put together a few threats with our bats, but hadn't scored either, so when I came out to start the fourth inning, the York bench started riding me. They must have figured the little show was over, and that the expected script would now play itself out.

Their lead-off guy came swaggering up for a second taste. I motioned with my head for him to get in the box, which he did to the even louder calls from his teammates.

I blew three pitches by him, just like that. Then, I told him to have a seat on the bench. He studied me for a moment, like he was seeing me for the first time, before walking back to the bench. The following guy popped out to third on a pitch in on his hands.

I knew the next guy mattered most, since he was their best player. He lumbered his bumpy torso up to the plate with a look on his face like he'd just eaten something insulting. He gave me a glare and spit through his teeth.

I looked him over and called "Three pitches" loud enough for everyone to hear. The guys behind me came alive, and the York bench jumped to its feet. The batter smiled and shook his head while digging into the box. Again, he spit through his teeth in my direction. It was loud and tense, but not a problem for me.

After agreeing to the first pitch, I made eye contact with the batter and told him, "Fastball." He snorted and dug in some more while I went through my wind-up, and I blew one in on the inside corner. Mr. Manners couldn't catch up.– His swing finished after the ball had already passed. I'd never thrown a ball so hard in my life.

"Strike one!" the umpire yelled. Screams continued from both sides. I took the next signal, addressed him again, and said, "Fastball." He might have been closer to this one, but not by much.

"Strike two!" was announced, and I could see the blood start to swell in the batter's face. When the ball came back, I tucked it into my glove and walked to the front of the mound. "You ready for the bender?" I asked.

He flared his nostrils and prepped himself by digging in his spikes, gripping and re-gripping the bat like he was strangling the poor thing. I stood tall on the mound, with my glove up high, just below my eyes. I began the wind-up with a small step backward and my hands rising, together in the glove, over my head. Then I dug a foot against the rubber and pivoted the other leg around the opposite hip, which launched my whole body forward toward the plate like a human missile. With my front foot in the dirt, I whipped my arm and body forward and prepared to release the ball.

I could feel the stitching between thumb and forefingers, and snapped the ball so hard it looked frozen, hanging high and still for a moment, fighting the spin, before the bottom fell out and the ball dropped two feet, right over the plate.

"Strike three!" yelled the umpire, punching his hand across his chest protector.

The poor guy from York stood there stunned, bat on his shoulder. I gave him a wink and walked toward the sound of applause.

Our team, pumped up by the showdown, didn't stop hitting until we had a five-run cushion. I mowed down the remaining batters without drama or danger, and when the last looped a lazy fly ball to our right fielder, Hamden Academy had beaten the York School in baseball for the first time in 10 seasons. I felt the crowd coming, but before the team could jump me, I searched the bleachers. Not too many people, really, for the first ball game of the season. Just a few, including Sammie up top and a *Bella Faccia* sitting alone in the front row. Brenda smiled at me, like I had asked her to in the letter. I should have asked for more.

After the hoopla, she was gone. It was late in the afternoon when we walked home, and the sky had turned as blue as the center of a flame. A breeze picked up, signaling the storm, and it dried the sweet sweat on my skin.

Chapter 18

That night at dinner, they made an announcement about my perfect game. The guys on our team, and the lacrosse team, too, chanted "Scholarship! Scholarship! Scholarship!" All that chanting ended when the announcements began about the upcoming wrestling match: the regional semi-final, to be held in our gym, the day after next.

Early the next morning, at my old Sunrise hour, I took a walk across campus with a stuffed knapsack that was practically all I could carry. Light was coming from over the hills and workers from town arrived on campus. A couple of students, like zombies, trudged their way toward detention. I pretended I was one of them, walking slowly, with my head down but, unlike them, I was alert in the early hour, my eyes alive, checking out everything.

A kid read a letter in the mail room, so I waited around the corner, in the shadows, until he left. With no one else in sight, I slipped inside and got right to work. First, I tore down the Support Wrestling signs, letting them scatter over the floor. Then I whipped out the stack of thick books I'd been carrying in my backpack and made a platform. With the spray can in my back pocket, I balanced on top of the books, pulled out the can, and sprayed in blue (our school color), as large as I could and as high as I could: ABORT

WRESTLING.

After checking out my work, I stuffed the books and the spray can back into my bag and walked through campus like a regular student. I went to the library, just after it opened, returned the encyclopedias and dictionaries, sat at a table, and pretended for an hour to be studious, though all I worked on were the next parts of my plan. I figured the first phase had been a success, getting those signs down and the new slogan up without being noticed. But someone had seen me come out of the mail room, and if they didn't know then, they knew for sure by lunchtime what I'd been up to.

—

The wrestling coach got up on the podium at lunch and made an announcement before the meal even started. His cauliflower ears burned bright as he tried to keep his cool, warning about desecration of school property and respect for tradition. According to this guy, jealousy was behind the "attack," and this type of outrage was a threat to our institution and would not be tolerated and yeah, yeah, yeah...

Word about the "attack" had reached me by second period. Some kid came into class and told everyone. I heard Meeks holding court in the hallway, and even before lunch, there was a steady line to get into the mail room. After lunch, and the announcement by hot-headed Coach Cauliflower Ears, people packed in there to get a load of what had been done. I had to admit, I was pretty proud. Less impressed was Trent McCoy, who walked into the mail room, right through the after-lunch crowd, and tore that bulletin board off the wall. To tell the truth, I had hoped he'd do something like that, since it made me feel confident about their probable reaction to part two of my plan.

The next part would be a lot harder to pull off, in a lot of ways. I needed help, too, so I looked across the room. Sammie wanted in, right away. He felt bad about everything that had happened, especially to Terence, and didn't mind risking his ass to try and make things right. I think he felt the same need to do something as I did, though neither of us knew at the time that what we were doing had a lot more to do with us, and the things that had happened to us, than anything else. What I did know was that having Sammie on board meant having a partner, a partner with a key to the wrestler's locker room.

On that moonless night, way past lights out, we watched from our room as the lights of the small security vehicle shined around the field, past the big buildings and finally through the Arch. We'd timed the trail four times and knew how much time we'd have to do what we had to do. Dressed in dark jeans and sweatshirts, zipped up and with hoods tied tight, Sammie and I crept out of our room, duct-taped the lock cylinder on the front door of the dorm, and skipped from tree to tree in the shadows along the path. In the landing behind the gymnasium, we entered that forgotten door that Brenda and I had probably been the last ones to use back in the fall.

Inside, it felt cold and creepy, and Sammie's flashlight shone on dripping pipes in the narrow corridor that led toward the abandoned locker room. We crept along like super sleuths, though we probably could have brought a boom box and cranked tunes, since nobody was securing the inside of the gym in the middle of the night.

After going through the halls and into the main gym area, Sammie busted out his key and worked the lock to the annex. We walked across the mats, into the empty, round theater, guided by the dim light that came through the small window up top. There were no windows in the locker room, so we hit the lights and looked around: high ceilings, soda machines, and a doctor's table; rows of dark blue lockers, full length, with each guy's last name on a plaque up top; a slogan up high painted across the cinder block walls, above a packed trophy case. Banners and posters and all sorts of memorabilia covered every other available inch.

It smelled pretty bad, being a locker room and everything, but not as bad as I'd figured it would. Sammie said that they had laundry machines in the back, and the manager had to wash their uniforms or practice gear every night. The floors looked mopped, too. There was a mile-high stack of clean towels on a table by the shower stalls.

I felt kind of powerful in there, those guys and their stuff at our mercy. A lot of damage could be done, from just tearing things down and making a mess, to writing something clever with my spray can, to doing something to their uniforms, like cutting them into bikinis before the big match. But that didn't sit right. Besides, we hadn't come for that. We had just come to make sure that the big ladder they used to get stuff hung from the Arch was in there. Sammie found it in the back, by the laundry machines. After we left, I poked around the main gym area, trying to find a way up to the roof. Then we went home and waited for the next day.

The new slogan caught on. Most everyone seemed to share it like a juicy secret. People whispered, not too quietly, "Abort Wrestling" as they passed each other around campus. Hands were slapped and looks exchanged. Notes were passed in class, and that day, in three of my five periods, it had been written on the desktop where I sat. "Abort Wrestling" was taking over. At lunch, people at back tables coughed it out loud, voices muffled into their hands.

The dining hall buzzed and the back-and-forth gossip seemed to hover right over the wrestlers' table. About halfway through lunch, the whole team got up and left together. When the last of them walked through the doorway, the room exploded with applause. The headmaster took to the podium and called for calm. But calm from what? You can't calm urgency. You can't calm community. People wanted to come together, and this was something we could come together about. We were just making a little noise. The wrestlers had, sort of, taken our school away; now we were sort of taking it back. Nobody had broken any rules, except for me, and nobody, except for Sammie, knew that it was me who had broken those rules. At least that's what I figured.

After classes, I was in the dorm, taking a leak, when Terence came into the bathroom. I'd seen him around, of course. He lived right next door and, as much time as he spent holed up in his room, he did have to come out sometimes. So we'd pass each other around campus and around the dorm, sometimes. He always looked mildly sedated.. I didn't even look at him when he squared off in the urinal next to mine.

"You think you're slick," he mumbled. His voice had gotten lower and slower. I wasn't crazy about talking to dudes when taking leaks, and he kind of caught me off guard, talking mysteriously and everything. I didn't say anything, just kept staring at the wall in front of me. "I saw your ass coming out of the mail room yesterday morning," he said, "when I was on my way to detention."

I peed faster, shook sloppy, fastened up, and made for the door.

Terence sort of huffed, in a mocking way, and put his eyes on me before I could walk out the door.

"I hope you ain't doing this for me, 'cause I don't give two shits about none of y'all."

I took a deep breath and thought for a second. "I'm doing it for all of us," I said, and walked out, leaving Terence with his dick in his hand. I wouldn't have minded hanging around and talking it out a bit with him. A lot had happened since that first day in the dorm, with that crazy scene in the lobby and then me getting caught dancing in my undies that afternoon when Terence moved in. A lot had happened, alright, but I didn't have time to talk about it then. I had a wrestling match to attend.

Chapter 19

I'd been on a school roof plenty of times. Back in the old neighborhood, I'd had to go up there whenever we ran out of balls. I'd get on a ledge by a corner window, where the school was one floor, then jump and catch the edge of the overhang and pull myself up. No problem. Once up there, I'd walk around on the gravel, fetch all the balls, and throw them down into the school yard. I was the only one of the guys athletic enough and gutsy enough to pull this off, and that was why my name was spray painted up higher than all the rest: I'd done it from the roof, hanging down by one hand and spraying DOMINO with the other.

Getting up on the gym roof at Hamden Academy wasn't going to be that easy. I'd been looking at the gymnasium complex all week, trying to figure out the best way to get on top of the wrestling annex. All I wanted to do was take a peek through the window in the roof, and check on the results of my plan so far. I could have done this the easy way, just by showing up, but I figured that, if things worked out as I hoped, and nobody went to the match except for me, it would seem suspicious. There could have been an easier way than getting up there on the roof, but I was in superhero mode, and doing it like this made me feel like a kid again.

I'd looked around the night before for the stairwell leading to the main gymnasium roof, but the door up top was locked, which was too bad, because it would have made things a breeze. The only other way I could think to get up there was through the maintenance area. This was the last compartment of the complex, and the cover they'd built for the grounds equipment was only one story. It bordered the woods out toward the fields, and I came around through the trees and stayed out of sight to make sure no one was there. I fastened the straps of my backpack, put up the hood on my sweatshirt, and tied it tight. To get into the maintenance area, all I had to do was climb a 12-foot hurricane fence. To get onto the roof, though, I had to ride a tractor.

They needed these giant farm tractors to cut all that grass, and I sat on top of the biggest one for about five minutes, trying to figure things out. There were buttons and levers and dials, and I didn't have a clue about any of them. I had a learner's permit, but had only driven our car around the block two or three times. The tractor keys were in the ignition already, which was good, because I hadn't even thought about keys. (I'd figured you used a button or a cord or something.) With the engine on, I pulled and pushed and turned everything I could until the beast jumped forward. I nearly fell off the back. I must have looked ridiculous, jerking around like that, but I wasn't there to win any farm boy style contest and, eventually, I got that monster out of the shed and right next to the roof.

From the top of the seat, the leap to the roof wasn't bad. The corrugated tin stung my hands and scratched my forearms, but I struggled and squirmed my way up there soon enough. The wrestling annex was the next section, and a ladder, mounted into the bricks, brought me up two flights. The lack of sound filled me with hope. I crept up onto the tar roof to the rounded window in the center. With my hands as a visor, I squinted through the glass until the scene below became clear: wrestlers on the mat and benches, coaches on both sides, a referee and a scorekeeper, nobody in the stands. Nobody except Rice and Santos in the front row of the balcony, paper bags of protest over their heads (I could tell it was them by the size and shape differential). Good one by those guys.

Instead of going back, I took the next ladder a few more stories up to the roof of the main gymnasium. The hills in every direction seemed endless, rolling over each other for as far as I could see. People walked around campus, and I felt like shouting out to them. I felt like letting them know I was up there, and what I'd been up to. Instead, I whipped out my spray can, went across the roof, and climbed down a few rungs on the ladder that led to the first section. From there, I hung out as far as I could and scrawled as wide as I could in the same style as I had in the mail room, but instead of the slogan, I wrote my name in gigantic letters: DOMINO.

I made it up and down all the sections, practically sliding down the ladders. From the tin roof, I jumped to the ground and landed with a thud. I climbed back over the fence and disappeared into the woods. By the time I got back around to campus, changed my clothes, and walked the path, people had gathered below what had been written on the side of the gymnasium. I bummed a smoke at the shack and admired my work. After that, I went home and got ready for dinner.

The wrestling team won. They'd be leaving in a few days for the national tournament. Big news, though nobody clapped when the announcement was made at dinner. Nobody except the faculty and some clueless freshmen. The rest of the large hall sat silent until a chant began. It began in the back and, at first, I couldn't make out what it was, but as momentum picked up across the room, I knew they were chanting for me or, at least, for whomever had started the rebellion against the wrestlers: "Domino!" "Domino!" "Domino!" "Domino!"

The sound bounced around the dining hall, and people began to pound on the big wooden tables. Not everybody was doing it, but enough. Not me, though. I couldn't call out my own name, and I felt a little uneasy, sitting there thinking as the dining hall echoed around me that maybe I'd made a mistake. I ditched that thought when I caught Brenda's eye. She sat a few tables away, not chanting or anything, just looking at me with an expression I couldn't make out. But she looked at me, and that was enough to keep me going.

Everything began to fall apart the next morning, right below the Arch. Sammie and I had pulled off the next part of our plan the night before, sneaking out of the dorm again and into the abandoned locker room. But something felt wrong as we crept through the corridor. My insides couldn't keep still, though I figured that might have something to do with all the prune juice we had tanked in our room after lights out.

Every part of the plan took longer than expected, but we got it done without getting caught and made it back to the dorm at about 2:00 in the morning. Sammie and I fell fast asleep. We even slept through our first classes and barely made it to the Arch in time to catch all the action.

At first, things seemed perfect. On that blue morning, a

crowd had gathered where the banner hung, and I smiled thinking about what we had done and how we had done it. In the wrestlers' locker room the night before, me and Sammie, side by side, the prune juice kicking in, our pants around our ankles, our privates hanging down as we squatted like two baboons in the woods, aimed our rectums into separate wrestling shoes Sammie had stolen earlier in the year. And the whole time, as we squatted and pooped, we laughed and laughed like no one's ever possibly laughed before. I really thought I might die, squatted down like that and laughing so hard. Relief and laughter and this twisted sense of payback made tears stream down our faces. We had both cried bitter tears earlier that year.

Afterward, with rubber gloves on, I carried the stinking shoes, carefully strung with twine. Sammie lugged the ladder across campus. Under the Arch, as careful as I could, I'd hung the shit-filled shoes from their most recent banner. Then we'd ditched the ladder so that it couldn't be used the next morning to get the hanging shoes down.

And that's how we found the wrestlers the next morning, in front of the crowd, trying to get their shoes down. Chester was up on the shoulders of two goons, trying to saw through the twine with his room key. McCoy stood behind them, hands on hips, breathing heavy through his nose. Chester's nose crinkled as he worked, aware of a funky smell, but too distracted with his arms stretched out over his head, way high up in the air. When the twine broke, Chester caught the shoes and was overwhelmed, right away, by the stink. He fell off the shoulder-platform and landed on his back. Shit from the shoes spilled all over his chest.

Some people laughed and some people didn't. I knew right away that I'd gone too far. Regret seeped in and sagged my shoulders. Another mistake that I'd have to fess up to and get punished for, but I wasn't fessing up right then, because McCoy walked into the crowd looking to provide some punishment. He grabbed every guy he could by the shirt, shaking them around and asking if they thought it was funny. He went one by one until people smartened up and got lost. I headed for the mail room like I had an interest in mail.

Surprisingly, something waited for me in my box. It was a big envelope with a logo on the front from Stonington College. What timing. I knew enough about college admissions to know that they didn't send a big envelope to say "thanks, but no thanks." I'd gotten into my first choice, a college on the seashore of Connecticut. Holy shit.

I tore open the envelope and read the letter about 10 times. I had earned one of those moments. One of those moments where joy fills you up, and you could scream or jump, just about blow up with happiness, tell everyone in sight — strangers or neighbors or friends — your good news. The mail room was filled with the faces of people who wanted to be anywhere but under the Arch, getting tossed around on a school morning by McCoy and company. They didn't deserve that. I did. So I swallowed my good news and left the mail room alone. The Arch had cleared out by then and the campus was quiet.

Later that day, low clouds crept in. A steady drizzle started in the afternoon and practice was canceled. I took a stroll through the soft rain, down to the falls. I sat on the bridge, above the misting water, and tried to get things straight. I'd been confused all day, feeling good about getting into college and everything, but bad about what happened under the Arch. I kept telling myself that those guys deserved every bit of what they got. I kept telling myself that they deserved it for being mean to Sammie and for what they did to Terence, and me, and our room, and the school, and everything else that made those jerk-offs such jerk-offs. I was a hero. That's what I told myself.

As the mist soaked into my clothes, the idea of me as a hero began to fade. I hadn't done what was right. I'd done what was easy. Making those morons look bad and turning the school on them had nothing to do with courage. Standing up to them, face-to-face, would have been better, but the way I did it made things worse. Those guys were madder than ever, and there was no way they were going to walk away or do the right thing. Now, thanks to me, bad things were coming. And I knew about bad things.

Bad things had happened to me, for sure, but because of those things, I'd been a jerk to my dad, and to Sammie, and to other people, too. I'd hurt the most beautiful girl in the world. I'd gotten so many things wrong and caused people pain, people who didn't deserve it. I'd lost my way. Big time. And as I sat there on the bridge, soaked through to the skin, I watched the rushing water get whisked away and wondered how to find my way home.

———

We had a game that next afternoon. I struck out three times, got hit by a pitch, and made two errors in the outfield. We lost 8-to-nothing. My head was off somewhere else, thinking about that school year, and the year before that, and the years before that. After the game, I tucked a ball into my glove and walked straight home, across the soggy fields and into the woods behind Montgomery. I pounded the ball over and over. Through the trees, I could hear the sound of voices raised, back and forth, that biting sound of barks.

The voices became recognizable when I reached the parking

lot: Rice's *fakadaka* way of speaking up against Chester's hillbilly twang. They went back and forth, up and down, and over each other. I heard a third voice, too, foreign and unrecognizable. When I got to the lobby, I realized it was the voice of Santos, a voice I'd never heard before. He screamed in Spanish, what I assumed were curse words, at 100 mph. Speed cursing must have been his sport, though nobody seemed to notice.

All eyes, about half the dorm and a pack of wrestlers, were on Rice and Chester in the middle of the common area. Sammie and a couple of other guys upstairs had come out of their rooms to lean over the railings and stare down at the action. Rice and Chester, nose to nose, or nose to neck, really, were attacking each other with threats and insults. Non-stop. Nonsensical. Their words had no meaning… just blathering that spun them toward fists. McCoy stood to the side, restrained by his teammates, ready to rip Rice to pieces. Veins bulged in McCoy's neck and forehead, his eyes about to burst out of his block head.

There were some calm voices, too. Voices of reason. Wrestlers reminding each other that they had a national tournament at stake. That they had scholarships to colleges. Guys from the dorm even called for Rice and Chester to back off, to go home, to give it a rest already. They must've been tired of all the drama. Tired of the effect it had on all of us.

Terence must have been tired of it, too. He stormed from the stairwell and pushed Chester right off his little feet. Just sent his ass flying across the common area. Tough day for that kid. First the stinky shoes, then this. He slid across the floor and all the noise stopped. The wrestlers let go of McCoy. He and Terence stared at each other from across the room. As they began to walk toward each other, I knew I had to do something to keep the dominoes from falling in the wrong direction.

When McCoy crouched and circled to his right, I raised my glove and timed him as he moved around, focusing on my spot. After a few turns, I had him in my sights. I made an abbreviated wind-up and then fired a bullet that caught the big bastard right in the balls. "Uhhh!" he coughed, and crumpled to the ground. All eyes turned to me.

I walked from the doorway to the center of the room. Chester snarled and stepped toward me. I bashed him in the mouth with my right hand. His teeth stung my fist, but I had to admit, having been dumped twice by those guys and intimidated by them throughout the year, it felt good to see them both on the ground at my feet. I felt powerful. That good feeling disappeared as soon as Mr. Wright barreled out of the stairwell. He didn't have to look too hard to figure out what had happened.

"Oh, Daniel," he moaned. "What have you done?"

My knuckles began to bleed.

Chapter 20

During dinner, which I wasn't allowed to attend, I went down to my old room to collect the rest of my things. The hearing with the headmaster had been scheduled for the next morning, but I didn't need him to tell me to pack. Out the window, over campus, the fading sky was purple as a bruise.

I made steady trips back down to Sammie's room, and only had the trunk left to drag when Terence walked in. He looked at me as curiously, as if he didn't know what to make of me, like he had on the first day of school when he and Mr. Wright caught me dancing in my undies. So much had happened between then and now.

"What are you doing in here?" he asked.

"Getting my things," I said. I tugged the trunk to the middle of the room until Terence blocked my progress. I dropped the trunk.

"You stole them shoes?" he asked.

"No, no," I said. "I found them, sort of, and figured they might come in handy at some point."

"The hell you do that for?"

"I don't know," I said. "It's kind of how I was brought up."

"Oh man, you trippin'. You know that?"

He walked around me to the back of the room and faced me from the window. "Everyone at dinner saying how they going to throw you out of here for this!"

"I know."

Terence fell onto his chair and rubbed his hands over his face and hair. I began to drag the trunk again.

"What'd you do that for?" he asked me again. "That was on me, not you."

"It was on all of us," I said.

"What?"

"All of us should have done something about them guys, not just you. You think you're the only person they got a problem with? The only person they gave a hard time?"

"I don't know about nobody else. All I know is they got a problem with me 'cause of the color of my skin."

"Maybe they do, and maybe they don't," I said. "I don't know and you don't know. What I do know is that you're the one who's got a problem with the color of your skin, more than anybody else, at least."

He called a horse and rolled his eyes. Then he tried to laugh. "Come on, man," he said. "You can't be serious with that. Ain't you read your history? Ain't you ever opened your eyes?"

"Yeah, my eyes are open and and what I see is a boulder on your shoulder."

"Awwww, shit," he said smiling, though he wasn't all that happy. "You too simple-minded to understand all this. Too simple and privileged. That's all."

"Privileged?" I laughed. "That's something from a scholarship guy who speaks French."

"Forget you!" he said, standing up.

"Tell me something," I said, staying calm. "Anybody have a

bigger problem with race than you?"

Terence held out his hands and bugged out his eyes. "Man, those guys been on my shit all year, man. And you saw what went down at the gym. They was picking on my moms. Picking on me for being black."

"No, they were picking on all that 'my moms is light-skinned' bullshit they must of overheard in the Can that day. They must have been there. You think them guys could have come up with that on their own? Who cares if she *was* white? Who gives a crap about that besides you?"

"Come on, man," Terence said. "You were sitting right next to me at that meeting. Those guys was on me from Day 1."

"They were pissed off because someone took something from them on Day 1, something valuable, and they wanted it back. And those guys ain't too bright, no doubt, but still, it wasn't all them. You were pissed off, too, about being here or whatever, before anyone started with you, and I know that because I was sitting right next to you, remember? And when they did look at you, if you didn't freak out about it, then maybe none of this would have happened. And even before that, if someone hadn't stolen their shoes in the first place, maybe none of this would have happened, and had that retard Rice not been so desperate to make things worse, and had everyone else not been so ready to go to all your games and support something besides wrestling, maybe none of this would have happened. And if I hadn't started messing with them, then, yeah, maybe we wouldn't even be having this conversation. But like I said before, and there ain't no maybe about it, the problem wasn't only theirs or yours or mine. It was all of ours, though the problem with race is mostly with you. Remember all that crap you had with the dorm *master* and the *overseeing*? About Denzel Washington. About your mother *not* being white. I do. It's been that way all year with you."

Terence sat back down and rubbed his head. Maybe he was starting to figure some things out.

"Were those guys at dinner?" I asked him.

"Who?"

"The wrestlers."

"Oh, yeah," he said. "The big one was walking kind of funny, and the other guy got himself a nice fat lip."

"But they didn't get in any trouble?"

"Naw," he said. "Well, they say the little one going home soon, for what happened before, you know, but nobody in any new trouble, besides you, that is."

That's what I figured.

"People gave them a lot of lip in there, too," Terence added.

"How?"

"They was sort of hissing and booing every time any one of them walked by."

"Get out of here."

"No, no, it was getting rough!" he insisted. "And they were passing out Sunrises like crazy, but that didn't stop 'em."

I would have liked to have been there for that.

"And then Sammie knocked a milk pitcher over the little one when he was walking back from the kitchen."

"Sammie!" I cried. "That's my boy right there."

"Yeah," Terence nodded. "He's gonna see sunrise the rest of the year."

"Ohhh!"

"It's still better than getting the boot."

"Isn't it?" I asked. "Isn't it better than going home? Having to walk out of here without finishing, giving up everything that could be coming next year."

He held my gaze for a moment. "Yeah," he said. "Yeah."

I went to the back of the room and stuck out my hand. "Just think about what I said, alright?"

"Yeah," he said. "Bet."

We shook hands, like real friends, and I was kind of OK with what had happened, though I still tasted regret, and it tasted like dirty pennies. Maybe someday, I thought, I'd figure out a way to avoid that taste.

———

In the morning, Mr. Wright walked me over to the headmaster's office. We didn't talk on the way. He spent a few minutes inside alone with the headmaster, then sat with me outside the office waiting for Pop. We'd spoken on the phone the night before, and I told Pop everything that had happened, just like I used to. He listened quietly, then said he'd see me tomorrow.

When Pop showed up, he shook Mr. Wright's hand like they knew each other already. Right away, the secretary said Headmaster Hurley would see us now. Pop and I were shown right in. Headmaster Hurley was kind of a young guy, tall and lanky, perfect hair and teeth, always smiling and slapping people on the back, cracking up at his own jokes. They said he used to be a Wall Street big shot who retired in his 40s and came out to Hamden Academy to keep busy. I didn't think much of him, either way, and he'd never said a word to me until the morning Pop and I walked into his light-filled office.

"Good morning, Daniel," he said like he knew me. He shook my hand from over a large desk. "And how are you, Mr. Rorro?"

Pop said he was good and sat down in the cushy leather chair next to mine. Hurley there made a temple out of his fingers and stared at us for a minute before talking.

"This is your second year here at Hamden Academy, right Daniel?"

I nodded and he kept talking.

"This marks the end of my third, so I've got you beat by a year." He laughed, alone. Then he went on this long blab-fest about himself. I can't remember the exact words, because it was boring and I was busy trying to figure out, the whole time, what the hell it had to do with me. Then he went on about how the school needed him and his business acumen to be competitive and, in order to be competitive, you had to play the game. That was the best part, about "playing the game." He went on and on about how Wall Street works and how those who make it know how the game works and all that. What a tool. I covered my mouth as I yawned. I'd been out late, sneaking from the dorm for one last mission. I kept yawning into my hand. Pop drummed his thighs while his mouth twitched. Hurley kept on until Pop held up his hand.

"What does this have to do with my son?"

"Well, sir," he said, sitting up and tilting his head. "I'm getting to that."

According to this guy, his biggest challenge was playing the game in a way that made Hamden more prestigious and whatnot without giving up what got us to where we were. He told us all this secret information about a football team coming and a new dorm being built and teachers from "top-notch" programs being added to the faculty so as to help raise academic standards.

Then he talked, without that same twinkle, about how important wrestling was to the school, to our reputation and everything, but that he didn't see a "symbiotic" relationship between wrestling and Hamden's future as one of those "elite" schools. His eyes got all bright again when he said that he had redirected scholarship funds and raised academic standards for student-athletes, and that he was doing all this other rigamarole to make wrestling less and less "influential." He said that fund-raising was the key to it all. I thought about the meeting Headmaster Hurley had had with Todd Brooks' father.

Pop held up his hand again and Headmaster Hurley, finally, got right to it. This part I remember good enough to quote, because it had to do with me.

"So the reason I tell you all of this is that, even with recent events, Daniel can be of service to Hamden Academy and Hamden Academy can be of service to Daniel. Now there's absolutely no way to keep him at school. The stunts were problematic, but not terminal. I even admired their ingenuity and effect. But he assaulted two students, in public, and for that, he must leave. That being said, there is a way for us to arrange his graduation through a prolonged suspension, as opposed to an expulsion."

"And why would you do that?" Pop asked, a wave of skepticism carrying his words.

"Because of Stonington, of course," he said. "And the interest they've had in Daniel since his perfect game."

And that's when Pop put his hot eyes on me. They bore into the side of my face as I tried to keep focused on Headmaster Hurley and all the noise he spouted, noise that buried me. According to him, if I somehow managed to graduate, I still might be the first Hamden student to get a scholarship to Stonington and the school could tout this as an accomplishment. A "win-win." I guess that's how the game is played in his world. But not in mine.

"Scholarship?" Pop asked me. "Perfect game?"

I must have forgotten to mention any of that. I tried to explain right there and then, but he gave me the hand. He turned to Headmaster Hurley, ready to share some of his wisdom, but I cut him off.

"It's OK, Pop," said. "I got this."

His face said he'd give me a chance.

"Thanks, Mr. Hurley, I guess, for the offer and everything, but I'm not going to Stonington College. I'm going home."

"Home?" he asked, like he'd never heard of the place. "What will you do there?"

"Go to school, get a job. There's lots to do," I said. "This is America."

Pop grabbed my forearm. "Sounds like you thought this through, Pal."

"Yeah," I kind of laughed. "Imagine that."

Before the ridiculous offer from the headmaster, I'd spent a lot of time thinking about my future. I'd go home to Queens, to our new house. I'd enroll in the local public school and graduate. Then I'd go to St. John's or somewhere else in the city. Or maybe I'd work a year or two and go away to college in a couple of years. Either way, I'd be home for awhile, a survivor of childhood. A survivor with a story to tell, and I'd get started telling it right away.

Headmaster Hurley sat there smirking, like we didn't get how the game was played. Pop sat up, with his forearms on Hurley's desk, and wiped the smirk off the headmaster's face by telling him he was a failure for teaching kids about privilege instead of fairness. He told him, calmly, about how *he* thought the game was played, with equality and compassion for everybody, no matter what. It was a speech I knew well, as I'd heard it a hundred times, but the truth of it hit me right then for the first time in a long time. And I remembered right then why Pop was my hero. And I wanted to be like him again, just like when I was a kid.

He put a hand on my shoulder and led me out the door. We picked up Mr. Wright and kept on walking. The only sound in the cool, dark corridor was of our six heels clacking the marble floor. As we walked toward the exit, Mr. Wright explained how he and Pop knew each other.

"Your father came up to see me on the day you moved in, and we spoke a lot about you. He asked me to keep an eye on you, and to challenge you, as well. That was why, on that very same day when the situation arose, I thought to move Mr. King to your room. I feel now like I put you in the wrong situation, and that I've somehow contributed to your fate."

"It wasn't your fault, Mr. Wright. You were right to bring him to me. I just blew it, that's all. All on my own." I faced them in the hallway. "Sorry I let you guys down and everything. I know you've been looking out for me and, you know, I'm a moron, but I was trying to do the right thing. I was."

"We know, Pal," Pop said with a tight smile. "I'm at least proud of you for trying, but I'd be singing Sinatra right now if you would have used your head, not your neck, to work this out — understand what I'm saying?"

"*Capisco*, Pop," I said. "*Capisco*."

"Good," he said, stepping toward the door. "Let's go home. You can tell me about the perfect game on the way." He gave me a wink.

I pushed open the exit bar and motioned for them to go first. I followed, blinking as my eyes adjusted to the bright sun that shined on what seemed like every kid in the whole school.

"What do we have here?" Pop asked as we entered the swarm. My small group of friends met us first, Terence and Sammie in front of Meeks and Grohl, but I also knew the names and faces of many others who had come to say goodbye. I walked through the crowd feeling the touches of those who reached for my arm or shook my hand.

I felt like a rock star and a superhero and a real kid all at the same time. Sadness sort of came over me, too. Not a hard-won sadness about what was, but a more hollow sadness about what could have been. I could have been friends with so many of those people. We could have had memories to take with us when we left Hamden Academy. Not making the most of those years, I guess, was my real punishment… that and the potatoes.

The people parted as Pop and I moved slowly under the Arch toward the visitor's parking lot. The mob scene extended across the meadow and toward the women's dorm. I could see the spray painted message I'd left for Brenda on their door — my last stunt, written the night before:

> *Bella Faccia!*
> *I Love You (10 X)*
> *DOMINO*

Brenda stood on the porch, in front of the door decorated just for her. She leaned way over the railing and waved to me. I figured she was saying goodbye. I waved back and turned away, feeling for a moment like I was going to cry. I passed Pop on my way to the car.

"Look out," he said before I reached the door. "This kid's got wheels."

When I turned, Brenda was halfway across the meadow, a jackrabbit heading through the crowd in a sweatshirt and jeans, hair bouncing and a smile as bright as her eyes. She never looked better.

She ran right at me, and I caught her under the arms and spun her around in the air. It felt like she had wings. Everybody cheered and kept on cheering and hollering after Brenda locked her legs around my waist and her hands around the back of my neck and kissed me like crazy. I didn't even close my eyes.

"Thanks for the note," she separated our lips to say.

"I was going to write the words to 'Thunder Road,'" I shrugged, "but it's too long and, you know..."

"I like your words better," she said, pulling me back in.

With my eyes closed, I remembered the first time we kissed on the bridge. I could hear the sound of the circling water, full of pain, being whisked away.

"You guys know each other?" Pop interrupted.

I staggered when we parted. Brenda stepped forward.

"Hello," she said, offering her hand to my father. "I'm Brenda Divine."

"Nice to meet you, Brenda Divine," Pop said.

"Nice to meet you, too," she answered, with a sweet tilt of her head. "I've heard a lot about you."

"Me?" Pop asked. "Get out of here."

"No, I have," she said with a gesture toward me. "And I can see the resemblance between you and little Dom."

Pop stood still, no wheels turning for something clever to say, his strong hands clenched at his sides, his face flushed from olive to almond. He looked proud to be my father. He shifted his eyes to me, holding them there for a moment before going back to Brenda.

"NYU," he said, noticing her sweatshirt. "That's some school."

"Yes it is," she smiled. "I start there in the fall. You know anyone who can show me around the city?"

They both turned to me. I fell over.

I swear.

THE END